Broken Rules And Other Stories

Barry Lee Thompson

16pt

Read How You Want
LARGE PRINT BOOKS, BRAILLE & DAISY

Copyright Page from the Original Book

MELBOURNE, AUSTRALIA
www.transitlounge.com.au
First Published 2020
Transit Lounge Publishing

Cover image: Ben McLaughlin/Bridgeman Images
Author image: Damjan Janevski
Cover and book design: Peter Lo
Printed in Australia by McPherson's Printing Group

This project is supported by the Victorian Government
through Creative Victoria.

This book was developed with the support of a
Fellowship from Varuna, The National Writers' House.

A cataloguing-entry is available from the
National Library of Australia: trove.nla.gov.au

TABLE OF CONTENTS

THEIR CRUEL ROUTINES

Over a number of days, Steven had been considering a recently recalled incident from his childhood. Or perhaps not so much an incident, but more of a scene. In the course of being revisited, the memory had begun to take on a troubling quality. In the scene stand Steven, his mother, and a third person, an unfamiliar man with coldly appraising eyes. The man speaks. He says that Steven has a delightful face. 'But his legs,' the man says, staring at the boy's scabbed shins.

'A nervous condition,' says his mother, looking shiftily at the legs. 'It seems more than it is.'

'Still,' says the man, souring his face.

Steven seeks reassurance, but his mother stands sideways to him, as if he is less than she'd previously believed.

The scene was isolated from its contexts. It had, in the manner of such recollections, been jolted into life by the trigger of a smell or a glance or a way of talking. For Steven, the defining characteristic of the memory was the mood of the adults: one of disappointment, of expectations unfulfilled.

And so, in the gloom of a Sunday afternoon, with nothing to do but listen to the clock and watch the rain, he described this memory and asked his mother about the exchange with the man. He asked if she thought she'd done her best to stand up for him against the man's disgust. Is this, he said, what other mothers would have done in the same situation?

She'd been listening to him carefully. 'I don't recall the situation,' she said. 'And it doesn't sound as if it has any significance. I'm sure you have your reasons for mentioning it.'

'The memory is clear,' he said. And he described it again, to show it couldn't be obliterated, ripped up and burned like an old photograph. He stressed the language that the man had used – 'delightful' was an unusual word choice, he said. 'A curious way for an older man to talk about a boy.'

'Just because you remember something, doesn't make it real,' she said. Something flashed across her face. 'Let me tell you about memory,' she said.

'I don't want to hear about your memories,' he said.

'I want to tell you about my father.'

'Why do you bring your own life up? I'm talking about mine.'

She went quiet.

She peered down her nose at him. 'If it happened, it's lost to me,' she said. 'And I have a good memory, as you know. Why are you asking about this now?'

'It seems to be important. I'm trying to piece together my childhood, and this is a fragment.' He gave her an even stare. 'And there are few photographs.'

His mother said quickly, as she didn't like talk of photographs or lack of them, 'No, I don't recall your man or his sour face.' She swept a look around the living room. 'But you've certainly soured the afternoon.' She smiled, a trick of hers, to sweeten her words. 'Let's have tea,' she said through the smile, a high note in her voice.

'He was definitely there,' said Steven. 'And more than once.'

She sighed. 'When was this?' she said, resigned, knowing he wasn't going to let it go.

'I was a boy, wearing shorts.'

'Goodness,' she said. 'Such a long time ago when you were a boy.'

He felt the barb, but didn't react, or tried not to.

'Perhaps he was a neighbour,' she said. 'Or a friend. I had friends, you know. Once.'

'No,' said Steven. 'That's not it. This man was disconnected from us. There was a formal air. You weren't friends. You wore a stiff coat, like a plain carpet.'

'Ridiculous,' she said.

'We saw him a few times. Maybe more than I can recall. I'm remembering all this now. It doesn't matter why. Things keep coming back. They wouldn't have mattered at the time. But now ... the coat, for example. I'm filling in the details.'

She thought for a moment. 'It sounds to me as if you're describing a visit to the doctor, but you've muddled the details. That's all. You search for mystery when things are straightforward. We were constantly visiting the surgery. For your legs.'

'Ah, yes, my legs,' he said, watching her closely, wondering if she might be casting her mind back to the sleepless nights, his scratching the rash until the thin skin on his lower legs was broken. Bloodstained sheets and pyjamas. Her wordless stripping of him and the bed. Throwing the soiled linen into a heap. Leaving him naked, to wash his wounds himself.

'Regardless of who he might be,' she said, 'I think it's unwise to be filling things in, as you say. You'll end up creating events that never occurred. I could fill things in, and then I'd have a whole fantasy life.' She paused, to check he was following her. 'A whole fantasy life. We'd all like our questions addressed. But we can't just invent the answers.'

'I'm only telling you what I remember,' he said. 'It must have come from somewhere.'

She twisted her mouth in a discomfited way, and sat up straighter in her chair.

'What's wrong?' he said. Now that she was old, full of aches, and feeble, she was no longer a threat, and in many ways her behaviour was amusing. 'You look like you've seen a ghost.'

'It's you. You make me wonder,' she said.

He pushed his lip out to mimic a sulk. 'Well if you won't tell me who this man was.'

'I don't know who he was,' she said, pulling a man into existence. Then, as if he'd caught her out, she narrowed her eyes. 'I don't know what you're talking about,' she said. 'You get me all worked up.'

'I'll make some tea,' he said, standing, and drawing a line under the conversation for the time being.

In the kitchen, he let the kettle whistle for longer than necessary. She disliked noise, and he smiled, imagined her frowning in the living room. She would be muttering about it, under her breath. He knew her well.

They sat with the tea steaming between them. Outside, it was darkening already. It wasn't yet five.

His mother shook her head at nothing. But Steven asked her what was on her mind.

'I wonder,' she said in her high, sweet voice, 'if we'll still be doing this, as we are now, in ten years.'

'If we're alive,' he said. He meant her.

'Shush,' she said. 'I don't like that talk.'

'Well.'

'But in ten years,' she said, ignoring him, 'you'll be old too. We'll be old together. It's reassuring to imagine the routines continuing.' She had a tendency to divide and partition life. She often spoke of seasons: she was in her winter years; he, autumn. Still, she couldn't quite bring herself to talk of endings – she would approach the subject then shy away at the last minute, just when she'd been near enough to touch it. If you were to say to her, 'What about when winter ends?' she'd say that it was the longest season. This was another of her psychological tricks, a method of avoiding her dues.

He crossed his legs, allowed the slipper to dangle from his foot. He looked out of the window: the bare trees put him in mind of abandoned churchyards. He wondered if he was having a premonition; perhaps it was simply a clue to the rest of his life. Slippers and tea, and the company of the old lady. The air had chilled. There were storms forecast.

'I enjoy storms,' she said.

'They frighten you,' he said.

'They can sometimes unnerve me, but I like them,' she said. 'I always have. But of course you know better. You always know better.' She looked down at her hands, and played sickeningly with a knuckle.

'I should know my place,' he said.

She looked up and nodded. He smiled. She frowned.

'Maybe I do,' he said. He was talking about knowing better.

'Did you see that?' she said. 'On the lawn just now?' She was staring through the window. Her face was waxy in the gloom. But there was nothing to see. She had become comically jumpy in her wintry years. 'It's getting dark,' she said. 'Put on a lamp. No. Too harsh. Light some candles. And draw the curtains.'

'It's early for candles and curtains,' he said. He ignored her requests and watched the dreary tea cooling. He wished for noisy activity, some reminder that an elsewhere existed beyond this room. He knew it did. He'd glimpsed it in the lighted windows of other houses, the flats nearby.

He would be embarrassed if it were known that his life amounted to this, the ticking and tocking of the clock. At work, he told colleagues that he lived in his mother's house, rather than living with his mother. This slight twist on the facts, by its quirkiness, didn't invite any further intrusion. But one time, Lorraine had ventured to ask, 'Is your mother still with us?' and he'd smiled, enigmatically he'd thought, said, 'Very much so,' then asked if her mother was also 'still with us'. Then he'd worried that he'd offended her. That he'd sounded curt, or smart. He'd approached her the next day, but she acted as if she'd come to an irrevocable conclusion about him.

The episode had confirmed something he already believed: that the more distant you keep yourself, the easier it is to maintain illusions. Tell people nothing, and they can know nothing. Let them in on a small detail, and you might end up revealing far more than was intended. But concealment was a trick, like his mother's tricks of the mind. He knew it was cowardly, to keep the truth from others. The idea niggled him all the time. But he couldn't face anybody else knowing the truth. And worse forms of cowardice were practised every day. He'd decided most people were cowards in their own ways.

'I've been thinking,' he said, bouncing his slipper on the end of his foot, 'about finding my own place. Somewhere nearby.'

'Shush,' she said. 'I saw it again.' She leaned forward. 'Something moved. At the bottom of the lawn.'

All Steven could see was the drenched garden, skeletal branches against the glowering sky and drops of rain on the glass. 'Probably a bird looking for shelter,' he said. 'Or a rat.'

It was her way to create dramas – it suited her to have a crisis circling. She did this to hold him close to her, in the house, where she wanted him. He was a prisoner, in a way. Another time, years ago, when hope's light was fuller, he'd told her he was thinking of looking for a place of his own. 'If you go I shall wear out,' she'd said then. 'We only have each other.'

Now she said, 'Go outside and have a look.'

He frowned. 'It's cold and damp,' he said. 'And there's nothing out there.'

'It's only rain. You won't melt,' she said. Then, shifting her tone, 'Go and see. To ease my mind. It'll only take a minute. Just a look around. Go now, before it gets fully dark.'

'If it's an animal, then what? It doesn't matter to us, does it?'

'If it's an animal, then it's an animal. I'll know. I want you to check.' And then the smile and the sweet voice: 'I'd like you to check for me. Go now. It's getting darker. Light a candle for me, before you go.'

Light it yourself, he thought, un-fooled by the frail vulnerability. But he lit two candles. He placed one on the coffee table, next to the tea tray, and the other on the sideboard, where a cluster of photographs might stand in other households.

He went to the hallway. To get to the back of the house he had to walk around the side. There was a back door, but an old desk was pushed in front of it. He opened the front door and cold air rushed through. The rain was heavier than he'd thought. He grabbed his coat.

His mother was framed in the living room, dwarfed inside her stuffed armchair. 'I can feel a draught,' she called.

He checked for his keys, then closed the door. He heard her voice from inside. The words weren't clear, but she would be wondering aloud why he always felt it necessary to slam doors. The street lamps were coming on. The slanting rain was lit by the neon glare. Pulling his coat around him, slippers squelching, he walked to the corner of the laneway at the side of the house.

Opposite were the lighted windows of the housing commission flats. In one of them, later on, the shirtless young man would begin to lift weights. Steven watched him sometimes, in the evenings, from the bathroom window, with the lights off. Watched him as he lifted and preened and occasionally admired himself in an unseen mirror.

The streetlights didn't reach to here. He should have brought the torch. He coughed a warning of approach to anyone who might be secluded in the wet shadows. Groups of teenagers from the flats sometimes congregated nearby. But the only sound was the plinking of dripping water from a broken gutter.

The garden gate was padlocked. He levered himself up at the greasy wall to peer over the top. Nothing was awry. He could turn around and go back inside, but his mother would want to see him in the garden, or else she would go on about it all night, and there'd be no rest; every noise would be accompanied by her fussing and shifting. He unlocked the gate and stood at the living-room window.

She was sitting in the flickering candlelight with her hands in her lap. Worrying her fingers, the way she worried their lives. If not for her, it would be rather a pretty picture, with the candles twinkling orange in the dark room.

Then she sat upright. She looked like a wild animal, alert to threats. She pushed herself out of her chair and he thought she might be about to walk to the window. But she stood with her hands clasped in front of her stomach.

He had a mischievous idea gambolling in his head. He would stare in, arms at his sides, and she'd become unsettled. He wouldn't move. She'd draw the curtains, maybe. No, she wouldn't. She'd be too afraid to walk to the window, nearer to the uncertainty. She'd leave the room, go to the kitchen, turn all the lights on. And she'd sit at the small table where they ate their meals night after night; she'd look from the yellow walls to her hands twisting like a nest of snakes on the tabletop. She would stay there a while, and hope he was playing games and wait for him to come back inside. With each second he didn't show, she'd grow more afraid.

He could stroll around the block, taking his time. And when he arrived back inside she'd tell him how she'd become bored with looking at him outside in the garden. 'You weren't scared, then?' he'd say, and she'd laugh, but it would be hollow laughter and he'd know the truth.

He licked his lips for a wet shine, and exposed his teeth, and widened his eyes into a dead stare, just to get her going even more. But as he stared, teeth bared, eyes agape, arms hanging lifeless at his sides, his mother came closer to the window. At first she was peering to the left of his face, to a point over his shoulder, as if trying to make sense of the space behind him. And then her hands came up from her belly to her chest, and her mouth fell open, and her eyes also began to widen slowly. She brought one of her hands up from her chest to her face. Her fingers covered her mouth, and she started to back away.

Without turning to follow her gaze, he ran to the gate, banged it shut behind him, fiddled with the lock, but it was dark, and his hands were cold and wet and the mechanism was stiff and slimy from years of rain and rusting, so he left it, left it open. Get it later, in the morning when it's light. It'll be okay tonight, just one night. He ran along the laneway, quickly, must get in from the cold, slippers flapping and tripping him in the wet, eyes stinging from the slanting freezing rain, not daring to look behind. Don't look, don't look; it doesn't exist if you don't see it. Don't look, keep running. And all the time a strange sound carrying from somewhere, an interior sound, high and light, distant and fragile in the damp air, repeating over and over, like the incomprehensible cackle of a deranged seabird.

THE MINISTRY MAN

I was fourteen when the ministry men arrived at my school. We were briefed about their visit: the men were coming to observe us, they would be taking notes, we should continue as normal and act as if they weren't there. For a week one of them sat at the back of my classroom, directly behind my desk, so that during periods of reading or writing or quiet contemplation I would hear him sigh or shift in his chair.

He was young for a government man, slim and graceful. His black suit hugged the contours of his body, and he wore it with a white shirt and skinny red tie. I would turn occasionally to look at him, but this was awkward as I had no reason to look, and so each time I turned I was revealing a secret impulse.

He sat with his legs crossed at the knee, making notes on a large pad which he carried about in his briefcase. The briefcase was a burnished reddish-brown, the colour of a fox, and scratched, its straps always dangling open when he carried it. He smelled of a light soapy cologne.

In the week he was there, I had only one real interaction with the ministry man. It happened after school on the Thursday afternoon. I was in the car park opposite school, smoking and watching the gates. The ministry man came out of the gates. I recognised him straight away. He checked to the left and the right, and then crossed the road. He'd removed his jacket, and it was folded over his arm. His line was directly towards where I stood. I felt sure he would recognise me from the classroom, and in the time it took for him to draw close I began to develop an idea that he might be coming over especially to speak with me. About what, the fantasy didn't inform me, but I decided it must be on some friendly business and that I had no reason to feel any concern.

I drew smoke deep into my lungs, enjoyed its familiar surge, and watched the ministry man make an unhurried path across the car park. A gentle breeze filled with spring-like promises of salt tackiness and warm seas and beaches was playing at my fringe.

I was disappointed that my cigarette was almost finished. I drew on the last of it, right to the filter, chemical-tasting and harshly hot; when I was sure he was watching, I dropped it to the ground and made a show of crushing it with my shoe. I put my hands into my pockets and touched the tops of my legs through the linings for reassurance.

The ministry man approached and I smiled. This smile felt complicit, like an agreement or understanding. I was allowing him to know certain things about me: that I smoked, that I hung around after school on my own. These were activities which for my mother might signal the beginnings of a troubled career; for that reason, I preferred to keep them hidden from her.

He didn't return my smile, and seemed about to walk by. I thought perhaps I'd read him wrong, and that he might consider reporting my activities to someone in authority at school the following morning. But then he stopped and looked at the ground as if searching for something dropped. Then, 'It's Steven, isn't it?' he said.

I nodded.

He offered his hand, and there was a pause of uncertainty in which I could think of nothing to say. I was relying on him to fill in the gaps. He didn't. We gazed at each other. His sunglasses were tinted by grey so faint that I could make out details of his eyes beyond my own reflections in the lenses. His face was a captivating composition of contrasts: milky pale skin flecked with coal-dust stubble at his jaw; full fruit-red lips; blue-black hair that shone like a pool of spilled ink. He'd slicked his hair down so that it was immobile in the breeze. I didn't allow my gaze to fall any lower than his tie knot. The knot, I admired, was impeccably centred and formed.

The time stretched between us like a slow elastic. 'Well,' he said, eventually, 'have a good evening. I'll see you tomorrow morning in class.'

I realised that I was still holding on to his hand, and pulled away, and a mirthful expression broke and spread over his face, easing the situation.

I watched him to the corner, his briefcase straps flapping as he walked. His black pants had the shine of wear and were taut across his backside. It was appropriate and effective on him. When he'd rounded the corner and gone out of sight, I jammed my hands deeper into my pockets. All that remained of the man was a fragrant tang of soap.

By the following week he had gone from the school along with his colleagues, their work completed. I invested, in the time that followed their departure, a great deal of energy into the recollection and exploration of that single brief encounter with the ministry man. I expanded and embellished the event, and attributed significance to every detail, however slight.

I pictured the two of us together in my room. It had been necessary for him to come over to my house, as part of his duties, to examine the home life of a student. He wanted to see where and how I did my homework. Comfortable in my now familiar presence, he stretched out on the bed, took off his shoes, and made notes while I worked. After a while he loosened his tie and dozed. As he dozed, I approached the bed. I gazed at my pillow, saw his face in the folds of fabric, whispered hotly into his ear. I placed my hand onto the pillow and kissed the back of it, closing my eyes, savouring the sensation, and pulling at the soft skin with hungry lips.

Over time, the fantasies became more intricate. One night when my homework assignments were completed, my mother insisted he join us for dinner. We talked, the three of us. And how we laughed! It grew late. 'Goodness, look at the time,' my mother said. 'Won't you please stay over? Steven won't mind sharing his room.' I rehearsed this particular night many times. There were endless possibilities. We went to my bedroom together, side by side, my mother smiling at us from the end of the hallway, and I closed my door and watched as the ministry man undressed to his underwear. I undressed slowly, trying to exhibit an appropriate shyness. I explained that I was accustomed to sleeping bare, and I hoped he wouldn't mind. Or he wasn't wearing any underpants, and undressed without care or explanation, standing stark naked while he slowly folded his clothes.

On it went. I knew I was exploring alleys where madness lurked, and told myself that all this was a one off, for a short time, an indulgence. I was, I see now, like an addict swearing off their substance after just one more session of use.

The fantasies persisted. I invented an entire life for him. His name was Christopher. He lived alone near the harbour in the city. He took frequent lovers. I imagined him waking in the mornings, checking the clock on his nightstand in the silver light of an urban dawn. As he watched the sleeping person beside him and tried to figure them out, I also tried to get a handle on their identity. Sometimes this sleeper was strikingly similar to me. Christopher unfolded himself carefully and considerately from the bed and its guest. Creaking gingerly across the floorboards, half asleep, finding the bathroom, he discharged a strong and quiet morning stream against the side of the toilet bowl. I tried to get a good look at his penis, at its length and girth, texture and colour and terrain, and to see how he handled it in his gentle slender fingers. I sometimes wondered what he thought about while he pissed, and if, like me, he observed his stream as it exited the head, or merely looked into the bowl or at the wall.

One late afternoon I asked my mother about the men who'd recently visited the school. She was frying three fatty chops in a shallow pan over a high heat, and I stood in the doorway to watch her. She looked up briefly, to check that I was there, that she wasn't hearing things in the sizzle of the meat. 'I thought they'd gone,' she said. I nodded. 'They were working for the government,' she said. Then she flipped the chops one by one. 'Assessing,' she added, as if the chops slapping into the oil had given her the word. 'I suppose they have to account for the way the taxes are spent.'

I waited for her to say more. She didn't. 'Is the ministry in the city?' I asked.

'I don't know. Probably. It's somewhere.'

Over dinner I mentioned the ministry again, and she must have sensed a rat. 'What is it with you and the ministry? Has someone said something?'

I kept my eyes on my plate. 'I've been thinking about jobs for when I finish school.'

'Concentrate on your schoolwork,' she said. 'That's enough for the time being.' She was nibbling daintily on a chop bone. She placed it on the side of her plate and kissed grease from her fingers. An oily smudge glistened on her upper lip. Our eyes met, and she wiped her lip with her napkin. She smoothed an eyebrow. She offered me more bread. She'd start clearing away the plates soon. My mother didn't like to eat very much, but enjoyed a smoke after dinner, and usually had two or three cigarettes on the veranda before watching the evening news.

I mashed peas into my potatoes. She stood and wiped her hands on a tea towel. She paused, seeming to see something in the air in front of her. Then she cleared everything except my plate from the table, and wished me a good night, the way she always did before going for her smoke, because sometimes I wouldn't see her again until the following morning. I knew that when I returned from my walk, the dishes would be done and the kitchen would be tidy.

I put out the light, went to my room, and grabbed the cigarettes from my schoolbag. On the way out, I detoured to the back of the house. I could see her standing on the veranda. I went quietly to the screen door and watched her from the side. She was smoking in that unusual way she had, with her left arm folded across her breast, resting the elbow of her smoking arm on her left forearm so she was holding the cigarette near the top of her head. For a long time I stood watching.

And then without moving she said, 'I know you're there.'

I started, and went out onto the veranda.

'What are you doing, hiding in the shadows?' she said. She tutted. She was looking at the sky purpling above the trees.

I felt for the bump of the cigarette packet in my back pocket.

'You're a strange boy,' she said. 'Queer, in many ways.' She squinted, trying to figure me out. 'Oh!' she said. 'I don't mean that. Not in the way it sounded. You know what I mean.'

I didn't know, but said nothing. It was warm and still and sticky out there, and I felt stifled. I felt some faint premonition that this might be the time of my reckoning, a punishment for the things I'd been doing in my mind with the ministry man.

'This is all I ever really wanted,' she said. 'To smoke, stare at the sky, collect my thoughts, sleep easy at night. Not very ambitious, is it? Maybe I'm flawed in some vital way. I should have wanted more, perhaps. For both of us.'

I didn't really understand what she was talking about. Sometimes her meanings were hidden beneath strange, lilting, cryptic language.

'Tell me,' she said, 'what's with that government man who came into your classroom?'

'You told me already. He was assessing.'

'Yes,' she said towards the bushes. 'You told me he was well dressed. What did he look like?'

I shifted my weight. 'He was tall,' I said. 'And he wore a black suit. Nothing remarkable, but it fitted him well. You know.'

'No,' she said. 'Well, maybe I do. It was tight – is that what you mean?'

'It was tight, yes. Fitted.'

'I thought so.' She turned to look at me. 'Was he handsome?'

At first I thought she might be asking for herself. So that's what she thinks about when she's out here alone, I thought. I felt an initial relief.

But she raised her eyebrows, waiting for me to answer, and I knew from her expression that this wasn't about her. There was a wilful smile playing at the edges of her lips.

I'd seen that expression once before, that time when she'd seen me naked, not so long ago. I'd been twelve, thirteen. It had been during my evening shower time, after I'd been to the beach for a smoke. Sitting on the sand, I'd been dreaming of the usual, of climbing into a strange man's car and escaping to the city. And in the shower I was probably thinking of one of those drivers, or perhaps a boy at school, or someone else. I don't recall – it doesn't matter. I'd finished off and dried myself and dashed out. My room was just across the hallway. But my mother was outside the bathroom, arms folded, leaning against the wall. 'At last,' she said. 'I thought you were never coming out.' I covered myself but it was too late: her eyes had run along my body. I was red with shame and anger, and gave her a look as she moved past. 'It's nothing I haven't seen before,' she said. I went to my bedroom and slammed the door. 'Don't be an idiot,' she called from outside. I dressed quickly, imagining all sorts. She was in the bathroom for an age. It was an anxious wait, a torture of uncertainty. I grew progressively angrier. I hated her for seeing me, for being outside while I'd been unaware. For causing me grief with her proximity to my intimate desires. The toilet flushed, the cistern filled and gurgled, then a lengthy pause and the sound of the tap running. I imagined her fixing her hair, her gaze drifting to the shower curtain reflected over her shoulder. I wanted to go and check the scene, convinced a musky essence would be lingering, and that she would surely recognise the smell. Then I heard her leave. She went down the hallway to the living room, and I heard the door being closed. I went back inside the bathroom, switched on the light. The smell was of soap and damp towels. I looked into the shower area. There was nothing to see.

After that I made sure she couldn't catch me unclothed again. Not even shirtless. I wanted to place a softening distance between myself and the event, and the best way to do that was not to point to it or remind her of it in any way.

I was remembering all this as I looked at her now on the veranda. This is the same woman, I thought. You can't erase knowledge, and memories don't go away. She thinks she understands my life.

'Well?' she said. 'Was he handsome?'

I didn't want to answer, because I didn't know the right response. Any reply would reveal my hand. I couldn't trust myself to dissemble effectively. I hadn't yet learned the subtle tricks of the grown-up world. And it was too late to feign surprise at her question – I'd missed the critical moment, so I was trapped.

She blew a huge plume of smoke into the air. It was thick like chalk dust. The whole thing had a theatrical effect. I tried to think. She was eyeing me. I didn't like it at all. I felt behind me for my packet of cigarettes. Her eyes followed my hand and I thought she was about to say something, that she might ask me what I kept hidden there.

But she went back to her cigarette. She made a moue with her lips and shrugged, but I don't think it was for me to see. I think she was resigning herself.

She ground out the cigarette on the veranda, and toed the stub into a loose pile of others. She wrapped her arms around herself. She looked finished. More than anything, I wanted a cigarette myself. I visualised the act of taking the packet from my pocket, in front of her, flipping it open, and so on. But my hand wouldn't move.

'I'm going for a walk,' I said.

'Yes,' she said. 'Of course you are.'

I went for my walk, along the beach. I sat on the sand and smoked, looking out to sea. As usual I imagined what it would be like to go back onto the main road, and hitch a lift with a stranger into the city. But that night, the cigarettes didn't taste the same or have their usual lift, and the sand felt inconvenient beneath me. I wasn't able to give myself up to my imagination.

I thought back to my mother on the veranda. It was a strange sensation I'd had when I walked away from her: a small event that felt bigger. It was as if I'd missed an important opportunity; and though I might want at some point in the future to try to bring it back, I had the feeling it would probably never return.

TWITCH

We do what we're told. We keep our heads down and our noses clean. We go to work and we come home at night on crowded trains, barely able to keep our eyes from closing. Sometimes we attempt to join the dots and make sense of the way our lives are going, but it hurts. It hurts because it doesn't make much sense, so we tune in to the noise around us instead. It's easier that way. With no time or energy left to attend to proper nourishment, we cram our weary faces with pasty white junk. We iron a shirt for the next day, and then we fall onto our beds, exhausted, into fitful anxiety-ridden sleep, and emerge the next morning to repeat the process.

Except I resist. I grab freedom in the small hours, when others sleep, in random anonymous online interactions on adult chat sites. Cam-to-cam, C2C. I watch as men and boys touch and finger and wank and come. I take part, reciprocate, but I never show my face. And I keep my tattoo, my indelible identifier, hidden, angled away from the webcam. I cavort through this nether world, and it swallows up my nights. But I take from it a steadying sense of control.

Perhaps I'm kidding myself. Probably we're all kidding ourselves.

In recent days I've felt even this small uncertain freedom coming under threat. Since the heatwave started, three days ago, I've been meeting Fournier out the front, late at night. Both of us seeking cool relief from our stuffy boxes. When he sees me, he limps round to my side of the fence. Sits next to me on the step, smoking those cheap tarry cigarettes that smell like garbage skips on fire. And I'm there in my underwear, tight and white, semi-hardness outlined darkly through the thin fabric. I gaze at the stars, trying to lose myself in the scale of the galaxy.

'Be careful,' he said the second night, looking at my moonlit legs. 'Online sex is turning risky. The laws have blurred.' He said 'risky' like he was hissing. His stammer, that's all. But it helped put the wind up me.

He told me about the television ad. Then he sent me the link. It's a short piece. A public information film. It begins in a house-lined night-time street, and ends with a man and his computer and peripherals being taken away by an official-looking group in an official-looking car. Seized. The camera pulls back to reveal neighbours coming to their windows and doors. Curtains twitching, faces pinching. Fournier says it's been on every night for a week or more. Nationwide alarm has been activated. Millions of real curtains have begun to twitch in sedate suburban boxes. Eyes have started to shift sideways. We're all watching each other now.

But the ad is too short, and non-specific. What's the crime? There's something missing. It bothers me. Fournier says that's the point – it's nebulous.

A notion that he's part of the campaign, or in the government's employ, sidles up to me. I shove it away. But it keeps coming back, whispering in my ear, trying to dissolve my trust in him. In my deep places, I know this is ridiculous. It's a symptom of the times, of the fear that's settling inside us all. Really, he's just warning me. He likes me.

So I probe a little. I ask him what he thinks we should be afraid of. He starts talking about metadata. He sees me chew the loose skin on my lower lip, and tells me that we can't assume we're not being watched.

I told him months ago that the same men keep recurring on the chat sites. Same faces or bodies or decor. Then, it was just a passing observation. Now he asks me how it can be like that. 'If there really are so many online,' he says, 'why the same ones over and over again?'

He's right. It's mysterious. Over ten thousand people online most nights, it says, but sometimes I see the fat old guy from Malta with the tiny cock and the grotesque horse ornaments and floral wallpaper ten times or more in the space of an hour.

Fournier has begun to conjure shadowy figures that creep through my nightscape. He says his wireless connection has slowed. Something's there, he says, but it's not declaring itself. There are oddities in the patterns. He's learned the patterns, he says. That's all he's got time for these days — telly and computer. Sedentary pursuits. Since his knee. He straightens his leg and rubs it.

I look up, and wonder about a white blob in the sky. A planet or star, maybe, but it's so big and bright. It doesn't appear to move, but it's difficult to tell.

Fournier reads my mind. 'Satellite,' he says. Clicks his tongue and pats my leg with a callused hand, and heaves himself up. 'See you tomorrow night,' he says. He goes back round the fence. 'Unless the heat breaks,' he adds.

Fournier's full of shit, mostly. I'm pretty sure of it. But still, I weigh up the modem, blinking at me from its corner of the living room. It seems, briefly, that it could be a conduit between this house and that white blob in the sky. An enormous bank of electronic panels opens up in my mind, staffed by uniformed men and women. Reams of metadata are spewing out for interpretation by the computers. They're waiting for us to slip up. But what's the offence? I don't believe anyone knows for sure anymore. I slam my computer lid shut, masturbate quickly, clean up and then fall asleep. I dream of satellites that look like planets, and planets that look like satellites, and the whole galaxy careens and conflates, and I wake jangling and rattling, glazed in a cool sheen that smells of salty dread.

THE AMERICANS

To my mother they were simply the Americans. At breakfast, in the bright optimism of the Avenham dining room, she would say, in her low singsong voice, buttering toast, head cocked to the side, not looking at anyone in particular, 'Here come the Americans.' It was said in a way that suggested we might consider making some adjustments to our behaviour. Her expression would morph into carefully studied nonchalance. This would prompt me to sit up straighter in my chair, while my father, in his usual unflappable manner, didn't react at all.

My parents and I were always downstairs in the dining room before the Americans arrived. But I had a wish that one day we might arrive at the same time as the other family so we could have longer in their company and be more at leisure to absorb their American ways. I enjoyed observing them: the way they handled their cutlery, how they chewed their food, how they spoke to one another. They'd still be breakfasting as we were leaving to go back to our rooms to gather our belongings for a day at the beach. There was always the opportunity of dinner, but coming near the end of the day this event held less potential for a hatching of shared plans. I felt that if we were to spend more time together in the early bacon-and-eggs atmosphere, there would be a chance for the parents to suggest getting together at the beach later on for milkshakes and meringues and games of cricket.

They were a family of four, each of them fascinating to me in their own right. But it was the boy who especially captured my interest. He was unlike any of the boys I knew back at home. Almost as tall as his father, he moved through space with a steady athletic grace as if he were moving through water. I'd never visited his country, a place of sky-scraping buildings and grand monstrous bridges and graffiti-plastered alleyways and subway trains I knew only from the late-night police dramas on the television. It was as if this boy had jumped straight out of the streets of San Francisco or New York into the quaint seaside lanes of the south coast of England.

He had a look of not caring much for anything. His sister appeared to possess a similar outlook. They shared a peculiar facial expression, like grazing cows with no particular reach in life beyond the perimeter of their paddock. Nothing caused them to smile or betray any flickers of curiosity. I hardly ever noticed the girl looking at me. At times I wondered if she were even aware of my existence.

The morning the American family walked into the dining room for the first time, the air inside the guesthouse was shifted. Even before I'd heard any of them speak, I could see they had an otherness about them. They smelled of different laundry products, for one thing. They moved in an alien way. Confident, expansive, territorial.

Dave, the man who ran the Avenham with his wife, greeted the family and showed them to the table next to ours. He made a showy fuss of pulling out the daughter's chair and shaking out her napkin and placing it across her knees. She accepted his attention without a hint of acknowledgement.

'Good morning,' my mother trilled to the American woman.

'Good morning,' said the other mother, smiling like none of my mother's friends at home ever smiled. The woman spoke the way a character in a television show might speak. I doubt my mother knew straight away that the woman was American. She would have just detected a hint of something foreign. A not-one-of-us aspect to the woman.

I was in two minds about their close proximity. On the one hand, I wanted the family near to us so I could observe them freely and without any obstructions; but I also knew that having them so close would inevitably consume my energies, and distract me to exhaustion. And it opened up the possibility I might be embarrassed at some inopportune disclosure from my mother, about my lack of interest in sports, or my solitary nature, or my liking for quiet gentle pursuits. My feeble thirteen-year-old physique was always up for scrutiny, and I didn't want to be compared unfavourably to the alarming robust health of the American boy.

My mother didn't like the American woman. I could tell from the way her face twitched; invisible to untrained eyes, but to me and my father it was as clear as if she'd declared her feelings to everybody in the dining room. My mother developed quick instinctive opinions about people, and once formed they rarely changed, even in the light of overwhelming new evidence to the contrary. Other people occupied her thoughts more than anything else. Though she deplored this trait in others, she was what might have been called a busybody. Nosey. I used to dread the idea that I might inherit this unhealthy obsession. While all around us people were busily going about their daily lives, my mother was busily observing them. It never occurred to me then that my own family might have been material for somebody else's gossip, or that my mother would one day magically emerge to me as someone I would like to have the opportunity of meeting again.

My father was fastidiously deconstructing a boiled egg, and he raised his eyes to mine, and I knew he was thinking the same thing. We both knew that my mother thought this other woman too much with her loud smiles and her unrestrained arrival into the dining room, and the way she did this with her hair, and that with her jewellery. It would all become explicit later that morning, when we were away from the guesthouse.

Rarely did anyone come up to my mother's standards. People were too forward, or too reticent. Too mousy, or too showy. Too familiar, or too stand-offish. And the clincher, when nothing else was available to her, was that they were just too much. At this my father would say nothing, sometimes looking to me as if I might have an appropriate rejoinder. We both quietly knew it was my mother who was too much. But we'd never have dared to voice this, not even to each other.

Now at breakfast my father was chiming in with a cheery good morning. Then the other father came in too, so that all the adults were greeting like bells in a tower over the scraping of chairs and clattering of hard smiles.

I watched the American boy carefully throughout the exchange: he didn't look once at any of the adults. At one point he nudged his sister and then described a shape or a symbol on the tablecloth with his index finger. As she watched his hand, he looked sideways at her, and something passed over their faces; not a smile, more an effort not to smile.

The boy caught my gaze, and I couldn't quite read his expression. I hadn't seen it before on anybody else's face, and so wasn't able to interpret it. I still find it hard to recall the look at will, but I've seen it since. It was a knowing look, as if he were aware of what I was after even though I didn't yet know it myself. His look filled me with a mysterious tingling hope.

When the family's breakfast was well underway, he stood and went to the juice table. It was a rickety thing with a white cloth covering, two plain glass jugs of apple and orange juice, and a tray of overturned glasses. He helped himself to the orange juice, and drank more than half the glass while he was standing there. He topped up his glass, and put the jug, now almost empty, back onto the table.

He stood at the table, sipping, hand upon his hip. The chalky seaside landscape that hung over the table had caught his eye, and he took in the cliffs, the sea, the amateurish attempts to capture the dramatic play of light and colours and fix an impression of them onto the canvas. The banality of that painting was familiar to me, and I wondered what he saw in it. I looked closely. He was slim, but not skinny like me. His hair and skin were the colours of a baked cheesecake. His jeans were faded to cornflower blue, and snug, despite his slim frame. I imagined all that his jeans were pretending to hide. But more than this. I wanted to ask him about his jeans. I wanted to know where such jeans could be found. Had he chosen them himself? I wanted to find out what he felt and thought about when he chose to wear them.

His hairstyle was a long way from my short and neat schoolboy crop. My hair was nothing special and didn't invite attention. Except once in a public toilet from a man who asked if I would like to borrow his comb when he saw me drying my hands through my hair; I told him no, in keeping with advice from my father. My hair was dull, but the American boy's hair cascaded lustrously to his shoulders. He had a habit of moving it away from his eyes with his fingertips, sweeping it back and then down to the sides, behind his ears. He was doing this now as I watched him, and I realised he was looking at himself in the glass of the picture. I wondered why he didn't just get his hair cut, as it appeared to cause him so much trouble. I would pluck up the courage and ask him about this too, I decided. Here was a person I wanted to befriend. An opportunity was bound to present itself. Maybe we would find the chance to go and have an ice-cream or a milkshake together, just the two of us.

Dave came out from the kitchen, smiling at the assembled guests. He noticed the almost empty juice jug and picked it up and looked at it as if he'd never seen it before. Then he took it away, back into the kitchen, and it didn't return to the table that morning as far as I knew.

***

Over the next few days, it was the mystery of the boy's voice that came to interest me more than anything else. I couldn't imagine him speaking. I wanted to experience his sound, his American accent, to watch his lips form coherent words and utterances. The thought of talking directly with him gave me butterflies, but still I wanted to hear him, to know what he had to say. I longed to spend time in his company.

But he occupied a very quiet space. It was frustrating. At some point he would have to say something, anything, if only to communicate what he wanted for breakfast or for pudding after dinner. But he didn't. Or I didn't hear him.

One morning, his mother brushed a strand of hair from his temple and asked him if he would like some eggs. He nodded and made a noise, like an affirmation, and then he looked up to see me staring at him. I didn't care that he saw me looking because it was the only piece of action taking place, so I had every reason to be watching. And so I felt the creep of bravery. We stared at each other, but he had added strength from the presence of his mother, so that my courage left me and I couldn't hold it any longer, and I had to look away.

Whenever his mouth moved in speech, his mother leaned in to him and put her head near to his lips to catch his utterances. Occasionally she hugged him close and long and placed a tender kiss onto his cheek, and a part of her lips brushed his. I looked at my own mother to see if she'd noticed this. I didn't want her getting any ideas. But she was buttering a slice of toast. She was always buttering a slice of toast. Her body was inclined faintly towards the other table, so attuned was she to the activities there. Even though she seemed otherwise absorbed, she wasn't missing a thing. I had an idea that she might be using the wide butter knife as a mirror, watching everything reflected on its shiny metal surface.

The boy looked older than me. This was confirmed one morning in our room when my mother remarked to my father that the American boy was well developed for his age. I was tallish, but very skinny. Lanky, gangly, awkward, whereas he was built like a young man. 'He's only fourteen,' she said to my father. Then she turned to appraise me with a pout. 'He'd make two of you,' she said down her nose, frowning, and I felt a sharp draining rush of failure, but also sheer embarrassment at this attention drawn to my physicality and its impending changes. A lot can happen to a teenager in a year: who knew what I'd look like when I got to his age. But I didn't want to discuss any of this; I preferred to keep my body and its development firmly outside the realms of family discussion.

Although it never became clear why they were holidaying in Bournemouth, we came to learn a number of facts about the American family. My mother had a technique for garnering information. From titbits overheard at the dining table, she could construct complete histories. Nothing got past her. She could have worked effectively in the intelligence services.

It turned out the family was from Boston. Boston! The very name was so American. I found it utterly incomprehensible that a family from Boston should want to take its annual holidays in Bournemouth. Surely Boston was a holiday destination in itself.

'Where is Boston, exactly?' I asked my father one morning. We were waiting in the lobby for my mother to come down from getting ready in the bedroom. We'd just seen the Americans leave the dining room and make their fragrant way upstairs. Dave's wife, Rose, was at the front desk, arranging pamphlets on local attractions into a plastic display case.

'East coast,' my father said, low and muttered in a way that told me he wasn't quite sure.

'Why are they here?' I said.

'They're on vacation,' he said, in a corny American accent. Then he looked around him. 'On vacation,' he said again, in a higher voice, this time without the accent.

'But why here?' I said.

'Why not?' he said. 'Bournemouth is as good as anywhere. Don't you like it here?'

I did like Bournemouth in many ways, and each year I looked forward with great eagerness to our fortnight away. In fact, I spent an inordinate amount of time thinking about the holidays during the rest of the year. But Bournemouth wasn't Boston. It was no America. And I would have been mortally disappointed to learn that it lay at the limits of life's adventures. I didn't want to hurt his feelings, though, so I just said yes, and then when he appeared satisfied, I added, 'But it's a strange place for Americans to visit.'

'A strange place for Americans?' he said.

'For a family like that,' I said, and I hoped he would understand what I meant because I wasn't really sure myself.

He looked at me as if I had said something awkward or difficult, and then, just when he appeared to be about to offer an observation, he glanced over my shoulder. 'Here comes your mother,' he said, and so I turned, and there she was, floating down the stairs as though she were entering an imperial ballroom.

***

We were in the town centre taking advantage of the late-night shopping, searching for holiday souvenirs to take back to family, friends, colleagues of my father, the neighbours at home. My mother had a scrupulously compiled list of gift recipients. My father suggested that once the shopping was finished we might round off the evening with a twilit stroll through the botanic gardens before the gates were locked for the night. Our holiday was beginning to draw to a close, the yearly fortnight away soon to be reduced to diminishing tan lines and a folder of smiling photos.

During our stroll, I spied the American family ahead of us. This was the first time I'd seen them away from the guesthouse, and I was pleased to know they occupied themselves with similar things to us in the evenings. They were milling around near a fountain festooned with garlands of multicoloured lights. I had no doubt my mother's sensors had alerted her to this development. We slowed our pace, behaving as a unit, taking the lead from my mother's stealth. She wouldn't want to catch up to the family, and I was sure she would prefer to avoid any interactions at all in these public surroundings.

Suddenly the American boy put his hand in the fountain and splashed his sister with a precisely directed scoop of water. She yelped then shouted something, and the two of them started running around like a couple of small children. My mother had stopped us at a kiosk to look at souvenirs and sweets and postcards while all of this was going on nearby. I took up a clever position at a dusty wire rack displaying the usual postcards of the town and beach and nearby attractions shown by day and night. I was able to watch the boy closely as he ran about. I enjoyed this glimpse of him engaged in physical activity. I occasionally lifted and fingered a postcard to add to the impression of absorption in the images, though I could have been holding a photograph of a Parisian street scene for all I knew or cared. I tried to capture the shape of his voice as he called out to his sister. But the sounds were distorted by distance and air, and the rush and gurgle of water from the fountain.

The mother joined in with the horseplay, chasing her teenagers round the fountain. But the daughter slowed and then stopped and dropped out of the game, so that it was just the boy and his mother running round and round. He chased the mother one way, then they swapped so the chaser became the hunted. The father and the girl stood next to each other, looking as though they had given up.

'I still think he's adopted,' my mother said, holding up a pointless glass ornament filled with layers of swirling coloured sand. I don't think she was at all aware of what she was holding, although she squinted into it in the way a collector of antiques might.

'I've told you what I think. It's none of our business,' my father said. He had shoved his hands deep into his pockets, and was dawdling aimlessly around the edges of a table stacked high with gaudily wrapped boxes of toffees and fudge, all ribbons and cellophane and depictions of lurid seaside scenes.

His response quieted her, briefly, and she considered the ornament, turning and twisting it in her fingers. I tried to picture her chasing me in these gardens. Round the fountain, one way then the other, splashing and laughing. But the image wouldn't come. It was impossible to imagine my mother high or carefree or reckless in blue jeans.

***

The next night, the Americans didn't appear at dinner and my mother kept going on about how they would miss it altogether if they didn't hurry.

'Maybe they've gone out to eat,' my father said, gnawing at the stubborn meat on the bone of a lamb chop. 'Don't you sometimes feel like trying something different?'

'But they've paid for dinner here,' said my mother, being an all-inclusive type.

My father dropped the bone onto his plate and it made a hollow clatter.

Dessert arrived. I was having ice-cream with chopped nuts and chocolate syrup. My parents had asked for the cheese board. On this trip my father had developed a liking for an unusual Danish cheese striated with blue veins, and now he was arranging some of this onto a cream cracker. My mother glowered as if he were enjoying the cheese out of a desire to be contrary.

Just then, the American family burst into the dining room. The son wasn't with them. It was just short of eight o'clock, and by this time the dinner performance was usually over.

My mother picked up the salt cellar, inclined it towards the ceiling lights, and gazed into it, rolling it round in her fingers as if seeking a fortune inside the grains.

'Are we too late?' the mother crooned to Dave.

'Of course not!' said Dave unconvincingly, wringing his hands and shooting an anxious glance along the corridor into the kitchen. My mother had said that the chef liked a drink, and I wondered if this had something to do with Dave's uncertainty. He guided them to their usual table.

Without moving her head my mother slid her sleeve up her wrist to consult her watch. She glanced at my father, her left eyebrow raised. She clearly wouldn't have shown the family the same grace.

'Terrific,' said the mother. 'We had a slight delay at the beach.'

'Oh,' said Dave, looking pained and somehow responsible for events at the beach. 'I do hope everything's alright,' he said, terribly proper and English all of a sudden.

The woman became more American in response. 'Nothing to worry about,' she said brightly. 'Teenagers. You know how it is.'

Dave didn't pursue it, and I wondered if he did know how it was, or if he might ask Rose about it later that night. He pulled out the mother's chair. The boy's chair remained disappointingly empty. I'd almost finished my ice-cream and the cheese board looked done with, so shortly we'd be off for our nightly walk and then I wouldn't see him again until breakfast. We were nearing the end of our holidays, and I still believed that he and I were destined to come together in some way, even if only to share a milkshake. This pre-destiny would have to unfold soon, otherwise I'd be going back up north on the train and he'd be flying home to Boston and we'd never see each other again.

Dave rushed around to the daughter's chair, but she sat down too quickly for him to pull it out for her. He shook out her napkin from the table and draped it over her lap, adjusting it with care. She said something from between her teeth.

I eyed the girl intently, trying to join her dots. I pictured her cruising the streets of Boston in her boyfriend's big red car. Driving with one hand on the wheel, the other on the gearstick, the boyfriend suggests they stop at Misty's for burgers and soda, 'and you can tell me all about your vacation in England.' She rolls her big cow eyes and tells him that the holidays were boring, and England's so dull. Dull, dull, dull. She blows a huge bubble of pink gum then pops it with a perfectly painted hot-pink fingernail, then says she'd much rather hear what he's been up to over the summer. And then as I realised that I too would rather hear what he's been up to over the summer, the images from Boston dissolved to leave just the girl glaring at me. I tried to offer an uncertain smile, but she was having none of it.

'I'll bring you the soup,' said Dave to the mother. 'Will your son be joining us?'

'He's getting changed,' she said, glancing at her husband again.

'Oh,' said Dave. He eyed the wall clock, which had edged beyond the sacred hour of eight. He went back to the kitchen.

The American woman said, 'Soup again,' in a distracted voice to no one in particular as she moved her cutlery into a more satisfying arrangement.

'I hope everything is okay,' my mother said. She was looking from beneath those formidable eyebrows, still holding on to the salt cellar.

The woman, caught masterfully off guard, said, 'Graham made some new friends down at the beach. He lost track of the time. We had to hurry to get back.' She looked at her husband, and I briefly thought that he might be the Graham she talked of.

'Oh?' said my mother.

'He went off for a while, that's all. It's not like him. We were concerned. Apparently I should learn to let go.' She looked at her husband again.

Realisation set in, and I felt a pang of disappointment that her son had been making new friends at the beach, when all the time I'd been on the same beach, available and only too willing to hang out with him.

'Here comes Graham now,' said the woman. 'Unfortunately he didn't have time to shower before dinner.' Her voice trailed off, and she looked down at the splayed fingers of her hand as though checking the nails were clean.

The American boy entered the dining room. Graham: what a wonderful name! My mind was flooded with a striking image of him taking the shower he didn't have time for. Concerned at where this might take me, and knowing I would soon have to stand up and leave the dining room, I tried to banish the thought by watching my father chase errant crumbs of cheese and cracker with his fingertip.

'Yes,' said my mother, drawing out the word as though everything had been explained. She watched Graham as he pulled out his chair. I wondered if she also had in her head an image of him standing beneath jets of water, soap suds running down his bare chest and long slim legs.

All this adult attention, had I been its recipient, would have made me blush. I examined Graham's face, grateful that he was the centre of activity, that it was okay for me to stare. Permission to gaze is a wonderful thing. Sparse whiskers were straggling at the edges of his cheeks. His hair, tangled and matted with salt and sand, stuck out at the back and sides. It all seemed so carefree and bronzed and Californian.

When he was seated, his mother said it was good of him to join them.

'Honey,' said the father sharply. Then he whispered a softer 'honey', but the echo of the first stayed in the air. He said something quietly about boys and wild oats. He was looking at my father, which seemed odd, but nobody reacted.

At the mention of wild oats, Graham caught my eye. I wanted to smile, to rescue things for him, to demonstrate an allegiance, but I felt stung and sore and it wouldn't come. He hesitated, just a brief pause, a hiccup in his insouciance, then he turned away and looked down, and I noticed then that he actually was blushing.

***

That night after dinner, the American parents were in the bar, as well as my parents and a loose collection of background guests I've largely forgotten about. The American teenagers had gone elsewhere, to places I could only imagine. Their parents were seated on stools at the bar, the way Americans sit in the movies. We were at our usual table near the door. I couldn't picture my mother up on a bar stool. I don't think she'd have known where to put her handbag.

The Americans were talking to Dave while he stocked the fridge with bottles.

'I won't be coming back next year,' said my mother.

'We're not the only guests,' said my father. 'It's just his way of getting to know them. It's their first time. He's putting them at ease.' He palpated his tie knot, and centred it just so, and then, satisfied, sipped from his glass of beer.

'Ease, my foot,' she said.

Dave held up a bottle of wine, displaying the label. The woman read it. Dave made some comment, then she laughed loudly, head back like a seal catching fish. Her husband's shoulders remained steady and square, and he had the guarded air of a stranger who happened to be sitting next to her.

I said that I wanted to go upstairs to read. My father handed over the room key. 'I'll bring you a drink later, and a snack, if you're still awake,' he said.

So off I went, with a vague idea to have one of my rambling night-time adventures. But I didn't go outside this time. Instead, sure that the adventure resided within the hotel, I started to walk upstairs. I arrived at the first floor, and Graham came running up the stairs behind me. I said a weak hi as he passed, and at first I thought I'd been too quiet for him to hear, but then he turned round and smiled, and something in the middle of my chest dropped out of my body. He unlocked and went into a room on that floor. Number 12. He left a trace of the cool evening in his wake. After he'd closed the door behind him, it held some element of him, resounded with clues upon and beyond its plain white surface.

I stood on the landing for some time. The light, tinged green from the carpets, had an underwater quality, and there was a reassuring smell of laundered linen and cakes of perfumed toilet soap. It was conceivable that if I was still and quiet, no one would ever come by and nothing would happen for the remainder of my life. I could cheat the rules of space and time and prevent the world from moving forward. As a watched kettle never boils, or a courted phone never rings, so a watched door will not open, a watched staircase produces no movement. It was a beautiful suspension, with Graham's nearness to me fixed for eternity.

But I broke the spell. I took a tentative step towards room 12. If I knocked on the door, if Graham were to answer, I'd say, what? What could I say? The answer would, I was certain, come to me. I'd be rescued by fate. I had nothing to lose and everything to lose. The holiday was almost over. I drew a fortifying breath, readying myself for the anxious unknown, but. But. My heart was fluttery. I felt far away, a faint impression, removed from myself and the scene.

I heard a noise behind me from the stairs, like fabric swishing through air, so I moved away from the door, retreating silently into a shady recess near the top of the stairs. The American woman passed by in a perfume of alcohol and fresh cigarette smoke.

She stood outside room 12 and straightened her skirt then knocked on the door. Nothing happened at first, but she was patient and didn't bother knocking again. Eventually the door opened. She said something. A radio's faint music came from inside the room. Then Graham stepped forward, appearing in the doorway. He was shirtless, and a white guest towel was secured tight around his hips so low as to reveal the line of the top of his pubic hair. There were drops of water on his chest. His hair was black with wetness and slicked away from his face.

His mother was talking, but I couldn't make out what was being said. He looked alternately from her face to the carpet at his feet. He kept fiddling with a tendril of his damp hair, playing it away as it tumbled over his face. As he lifted his arm to do this, there was a flash of dark hair in his armpit. Bushy, manly, raw and exciting, a public display of his body's changes. I wondered when, if ever, hair would begin to grow under my arms.

She reached out, as if she were about to take his hand. But instead, she put two fingers inside the top of the towel and pulled him towards her. She kissed him, on the cheek, near to his ear, the way I'd seen her do in the dining room. They came apart, then kissed again. He stepped back into the doorway, and said something. He looked down. She placed her hand onto his upper arm and he looked up. He said something that sounded like 'soldiers', then she nodded then walked away, and he closed the door.

She saw me standing there, but didn't speak or register any surprise. She bumped into the banister and went down the stairs, back to the bar, into the activity.

It was now just me and Graham on opposite sides of a closed door. Watching all of this had loosened something inside me. My mother had a concern, often voiced to her friends, to neighbours, teachers, to anyone prepared to listen, that I wasn't a mixer, that I didn't take part in things and had no interest in socialising with other children my age. She talked it up into a problem. She was right in her categorisation but wrong in her attitude. I had chosen to be that way. I had limited interest in the company of other children. But I recognised that here was a chance to put that right, to make an effort, to get myself out there and reach towards a boy of my age, or near to my age. Hands across the water, a friendship for life. Perhaps.

I walked up to his door. Tell me about America, I thought. That's all I had to say. Tell me about Boston. I want to hear all about the streets of your city. Its smells, sounds, its people. Your friends, tell me what they look like. Tell me all about your friends, and what you talk of with them, and describe the things you think of when you turn the lights out at night.

And so, with this in mind, I tapped on the door, three times, almost as if I didn't want anyone to answer, but each knock was slightly louder than the last. Because in truth I did want someone to answer, even though I knew that the easiest, the least challenging outcome would have been for no one to respond.

There was no answer, so I tried again, three knocks, slightly louder this time. In the middle of the door was a tiny peephole like a bubble, and I fancied that he might be looking through it, spying the distortion of my face, trying to figure it out and thinking that perhaps whoever it was had come to the wrong room.

My enquiry wasn't answered. I counted down from ten while I was standing there, believing he might come to the door before I got to one. Then I counted down again, slowly, slowly, certain that something had to happen after a countdown. Something must happen. Life depended on events occurring. I considered knocking again. Just one more time. I think about it sometimes, and I wonder what might have been had I tried that third time.

GRAY

Afterwards, I dressed quickly while he watched from the bed. Then I examined the framed photographs he'd placed on the nightstand earlier. To help me out, he'd said as he arranged them. Black-and-white images of him from a more youthful time. In some he was alone; in others with friends, boyfriends; androgynous groups at the beach, in backyards.

I picked up one of the pictures: a solitary figure, firm and brimming, on a seawall, a bare knee drawn up to his chin. Brilliantined hair, cut in a similar style to mine. 'You?' I said, inclining the frame towards him. He nodded. 'Handsome,' I said. 'Who took the picture?' He shook his head, said he didn't remember, that it was probably a friend.

He got out of the bed and dressed with slow care into a light grey suit. The suit was much too big for him. It did him no favours, and put years on him. It gave him the lonely look of one who's lost all sense of self-awareness, and who no longer has reliable friends to provide kind advice against wearing pale grey suits. On closer inspection, and I felt this was okay to do, I noticed that the suit, like him, was frayed in parts, and had tidemarks of greasy grime at the inner cuffs and on the top of the collar. But it had possibly, based on the photographic evidence, been a good fit at one time.

As I fingered the fabric he watched patiently, and this felt more intimate than anything that had happened in the bed. I felt solicitude for the frame rattling inside the garment, and I didn't want to leave the old man just yet.

He said he was going for his walk to the park, and I followed him, down in the elevator, then by his side, and he didn't seem to find this unusual. As we walked he told me he was accustomed to taking coffee in the park every morning, unless the weather was wet or cold.

We wandered among the early morning activity of shops and cafes preparing for the day ahead. A delivery driver was unloading boxes from the back of a van. He looked at the old man and smiled at me. When we'd passed the van, the old man said, 'He thought you were my son.'

I peered sideways. His expression was serious. Grandson more like, I thought.

'Sometimes,' he said, 'I come out for a walk even if it's raining, as long as it's not too cold. I've never really minded the rain.'

We stopped at the gates to the park. He told me we'd arrived. I had no bookings for the rest of that day, so I suggested I might come in and sit with him a while.

He hesitated. 'I can't pay you for this,' he said under his breath, as if someone might be around to hear. 'What's left has to last me for the rest of the week.'

I told him no, no, it was okay, I just wanted to spend some time in the park.

He led the way through the gates and across the unkempt grass to a stone and wooden bench beneath a spreading tree. It was a peaceful setting, mossy and secluded. No one else in the park, apart from us and the birds. I asked him about the tree, what type it was. He shook his head. He had no idea. I was surprised he didn't know.

After a while, 'About now,' he said, 'would normally be the time for my coffee.'

I told him I'd get coffee for both of us.

'I wasn't suggesting...' he said, making moves to find his wallet. I touched his hand, stopped his search, refused his money.

I went to the cafe he'd indicated outside the park and across the road. He said they made good coffee in there. 'In parts of Italy,' he said, 'they would struggle to make it so well.'

At the cafe I joined a line of three customers. While I waited, I christened the old man Gray, with an 'a', the American way, on account of his hair and his suit. Spelled that way the name seemed lighter, more informal, and was more like an actual nickname; short, perhaps, for Grady or Graham or Grayson. Not that he would ever know this name I'd given him. It was a mental shorthand I was accustomed to using for clients.

I took the coffees back to the bench. Gray was as I'd left him, occupied with being seated, listening to the birds, watching the park.

The coffee turned out as he'd described.

The morning was getting warmer. I hadn't had any breakfast. I asked Gray if he was hungry. He said he rarely ate breakfast. He rarely ate anything. I said I'd be back soon, and I went to a kiosk I'd noticed earlier and bought two ice-cream cones. They started to melt as I carried them back to the bench, and they went all over my fingers.

He gave me his handkerchief to clean up the mess. He said this was the first ice-cream he'd had in a long time. I asked him how long. He said he didn't know exactly. He asked if it was important.

I shook my head. I stared through the canopy of green above us. A police or ambulance siren irrupted. I listened to its wail fade away, then tried to pick out traffic noises from between the calls of birds.

'Living alone,' he said. Then nothing. I cleared my throat. 'Living alone,' he continued, 'is, well, it makes a person forget things. How to speak, and how to be with people.' Conversation was like a muscle, needing regular practice, he said, and he'd become rusty. 'It's a long time since the last ice-cream. I don't remember exactly. Long enough to make a remark.'

He stared off to the edge of the park. Railings separated this enclave from the rush of the road. Without the railings, without the road, we might have been in some wild forgotten meadow.

'It's a habit, coming here,' he said. 'To the same place every time. Almost every time. Once or twice someone's been on this bench, and I've had to find another place to sit. I was annoyed, those times. Irritated by the person who'd intruded.' He smiled. 'I wanted to pull them off the bench, or at least tell them to go somewhere else. Silly. But this is mine, I feel.'

'It's only human to occasionally experience an urge towards something uncivilised,' I said.

'You knew this was the bench,' he said, serious again. 'When we came in. How did you know?'

I told him I hadn't known.

'But you brought us over here,' he said.

I told him he'd chosen the bench, and I'd followed.

He nodded. 'I must seem rude,' he said. 'You're polite. Well turned out. You make an effort. And you bought ice-cream and the coffee.' He made a move to get his wallet again. I waved him away. 'I have to pay you,' he said. 'I invited you. Let me pay for the coffee, at least. It would make me feel better.'

I told him again to keep hold of his money. I reminded him that he hadn't invited me to the park, that I'd asked if I could join him. If anything, I was the rude one, the intruder. Anyway, if it bothered him, he could buy the coffees next time.

That satisfied him, but only briefly. He said there probably wouldn't be a next time. 'I can't afford to see you again,' he said. 'Not for a long time. And I don't have a long time. And you won't come all the way over here just for coffee.' His eyes were full of searching, the lost eyes of a dog. I wondered if he might be asking a question.

'It's not such a long way,' I said. 'And it'd be worth the journey for the coffee.' There was a tone to this which I regretted. Meaningless, flippant or, worse, patronising. I pressed on with the point, though. I tried to convince him that I would come over to see him one day. But I was much too insistent, and knew, even as I was assuring and denying his words and believing my own, that I would never see him again.

PHASE

The summers of my childhood are contained forever inside a sunlit memory. They were the days of the long school holidays. Six weeks stretching, more like months and months, almost never-ending. The weather was always permitting, reliably kind, bright and fair. Drowsy, idyllic afternoons spent lounging in swimming trunks, sunbathing in the back garden. Dappled shade would creep across my skin, and I'd shift my towel into full patches of light as the sun passed benignly overhead. My recollections are infused with scents of cut grass from the neighbours' lawns and the bergamot oil lacing the French suntan lotion my parents couldn't afford but bought anyway.

Summer was a lift from the mundane. We lived, the three of us, in what I know now as a cul-de-sac, although nobody around there ever referred to it in that way. It was a neighbourhood of uniform terraced houses within a sprawl of council estates on the edge of the city. For the most part the neighbours stayed the same from one year to the next. It was a place of routine predictability, like a well-made clockwork mechanism.

I harboured a yearning to be far from those estates, far from their narrowness, away from the animosity and hostile graffiti blighting their streets. At night in the confines of my bedroom I'd pore over my atlas for escape routes, and dream the names I read on the colourful cluttered pages into vivid images of beauty. I'd hover my finger over a page, allow it to fall and press onto and feel the names of cities I fancied, of countries that sounded poetic and exotic, and I'd trace the patterns of their geography upon the paper as if touch alone might transport me. It was easier when the sun shone to pretend I was already transported, already elsewhere.

That summer, the second of my high school years, the radio was never off, and its music transformed the urban surroundings into beach and poolside scenes from Ibiza and the Costas. *Top of the Pops* burst weekly onto the television screen with videos of sunny boys in the shortest shorts and tightest swimming trunks. Long-limbed and pouty, they expressed deceptively uncomplicated lyrics about friendships and love and life on the dole with all the attendant joys and heartaches.

My parents half watched these chart shows with me. While I was feeling the ache of overwhelming desire, Mum would tut that the bands looked doped up to the eyeballs, and Dad would peek at me from over the top of his book and talk about the songs having been written in five minutes on the toilet. They were wrong to be so dismissive, although Dad's comments were always delivered in a winking half-smiling tone, like an in-joke shared between me and him. I knew that love and light and art were on my side, even though I'd always felt in some way at odds with the world. These lyrics and images were addressing me directly, exhorting me to thumb my nose, ignore, to rebel, be different, live the life and be the person I wanted. I listened to their messages, and wanted to be the boys while secretly lusting after them.

***

Every weekday afternoon a paperboy would appear at around three o'clock, making his way down the narrow footpath along the bottom of the row of backyards to take the evening paper to the Watson house. As soon as he'd passed I'd leap from my towel and dash into our house. There wasn't much time till he got to the front. Run, run. Through the passageway, dart across the hall, then enter the kitchen. Try to look cool, nonchalant, casual. Dad's at the cooker, spoon poised over the pan. 'What's to do with you?' he says.

'Nothing,' I say.

'Right,' he says.

There's a slight catch in his voice, and I look over to see if something else was behind his words. It strikes me that he looks a bit lost, a tea towel slung over one of his wide shoulders. And I feel a twinge of regret for the way I dismissed him. 'I just came in for some water,' I say, picking up a glass from the draining board. I take my time filling it from the tap, all the while poking my nose into the net curtains.

Then the paperboy strolls into the frame, confident and contained but oblivious to my viewing, and then he's gone again. Gone until the same time tomorrow afternoon.

'What's so interesting out there?' says Dad, coming to the window, stooping to peer out.

'Just someone I know,' I say.

'A friend of yours?'

I wish it were, but I tell him again that it's just someone.

'The same someone as yesterday?' he says.

I rinse the glass and replace it on the draining board.

'And the day before, and the day before that,' he says. He picks up the glass I've just rinsed and holds it in front of me. There are lip marks on the rim. He puts it aside, says he'll do it later.

I make for the door.

'Nice to see you,' says Dad. 'Thanks for popping in.'

I stop in the doorway, leaning on the jamb. He's got his head over whatever's cooking up in the pan. I look down at my legs, wishing them hairier, less spindly. Wishing I were not quite so skinny. Hoping that one day they will stop calling me Muscles at school. It's meant affectionately, I'm told, and there's no reason to think otherwise, but it gets on my nerves all the same.

He puts the lid on the pan and turns and looks me over. He says I've caught the sun. He comes closer, brandishing the wooden spoon stained yellow from years of sauces, and he squints at my shoulder. He touches the skin there, warily, like an inexperienced doctor. His fingertips are rough. The nascent sunburn tingles to life at his attention. 'I've told you to be careful out there,' he says. I inch the waist of my swimming trunks down to show him the tan line I've been working on. A cluster of pubic hair spills out. 'Be careful,' he says again.

'Okay,' I say. I've no intention of being careful. I pull the waistband of the trunks out and back against my skin, stuff my hand down the front and adjust myself. I want to head out to the garden again to catch the last of the sun, but I stay a while, jangling in the doorway.

Finished with the pan for now, he sits and sniffs and picks up his hardback from the table. He checks the cover, opens it and starts reading.

The pot simmers. Puffs of steam escape the lid. High summer, as high as it gets around here, and we're having winter food for tea. Dad's in charge of the menu now; in charge of the running of the house, of me. He slipped a disc a few years ago. He was in traction for ages, and then not long after his return to work he was made redundant. Mum took a clerical job at the personal credit place in town, and handed over the household duties. It was a smooth transition. That's how it seemed to me, or if there were any difficult negotiations, they occurred when I wasn't around. One day, though, I overheard them talking. He told Mum he didn't miss the work, not at all. The driving, the lorries, none of it. But the union side of things, he said he missed all of that. I didn't hear any response from Mum. I didn't hear Mum at all. It just went quiet. And thinking about it now, I wonder if what I heard that day was Dad talking on the phone to someone.

The breeze billows the nets into lazy sails. In drifts the smell of heat-baked concrete, and it mingles with overcooked vegetables and stewing steak. Beyond is pure urban decay, but within these endless afternoons, school finished till

September, none of that matters. It's easy to craft a gulf between the outside and the world within these walls.

Without looking up he says I'm making him nervous standing there. Nothing ever makes him nervous so I stay where I am. He closes the book over a finger and pulls another chair out from the table.

We sit and sit, and that's all, and it's enough for us.

There's something I'd like to talk about, but not now, not yet. I want to ask him about phases. Last term, we were having sex education. One morning we were shown a thrillingly graphic film about puberty, followed by a talk. Some boys, we were told, and probably girls too, though I don't recall hearing that, would go through a phase of same-sex attraction during their adolescence. It was a normal feature of growing up. At this announcement I'd blushed and, already aroused by the film, and trying not to give anything away, I'd looked around at the others. Disappointingly, there wasn't a flicker from Michael Liscard. In fact, no one else seemed to have reacted at all. I wondered if any of them had even been listening, or had processed the information in the same way, or if I was the only one, the sole surveyor of this beautifully strange and fragile terrain.

The lesson had been reassuring. More. A huge relief. Everyone wants to fit in, and up till then I'd been worried about being different, confused by my feelings. But now it looked as if the feelings I was afraid to face were symptoms of a phase. They would wither. I was in a temporary state that had been licensed by my educators. I made a pact with myself to go with the flow. I might as well embrace the experience. At twenty-six I'd be getting married, headed for the two-children family life that Madam Sorina, much to the delight of my mother, had foretold for me one rainy afternoon in Blackpool when she read my palm and got so much of me spot-on.

All this is rolling in my mind at the kitchen table. Feelings, phases, the future. I've been wondering if maybe Dad had a phase himself when he was younger. And if he did, what did he do with it? I don't know how to frame the question. I'm not even sure exactly what the question is. But we've got a long time, the rest of the summer, it doesn't have to be right now. He's not going anywhere, and neither am I.

So I watch him read. The sunshine can wait for now. He reads a lot. A couple of library books a week. Detective fiction, mainly. Not my kind of thing. He says he likes to figure things out before the endings.

He turns a page. The paper makes a dry reassuring sound. I wonder if he's forgotten that I'm sitting there. Then he looks up and searches over my face. He goes back to the book.

He'll tell me, at another table in a different place, that he already had some idea of what was on my mind, of what was to do. That he was marking his time in the same way he would mark his place in a book, knowing he could come back. For much of that summer, he'll say, he was wryly observing the curious ways of his teenage son.

***

I shake out the towel, scaring a blackbird from the tree. I look around at the neighbours' fences, close by on either side of our small patch of lawn, then I slide my body into a comfortable position. I reach across and turn down the volume on the transistor a little. Lying on my front, desire straining and concealed, I writhe slowly, pushing my pelvis into the ground. I choose someone to think about. It could be anyone I use. I'm ruthless for the purpose. The paperboy's the most recent memory, but it could be Michael or any of the other boys from my year, or one of the elusive sixth formers, or my cousin Paul, or Mrs Dodd's son. Anyone. I've an extensive repertoire. Sometimes they all flash through my mind in flickering spasms, or they blend gently into a perfect composite.

I try to keep my eyes trained on the back door, alert for my father, but they might as well be closed because all I'm seeing is my own movie of legs, mouths, profiles, angles; legs, and the space and the angle between them, and the way they scissor, and what's happening inside the jeans or the trousers or inside the underwear as those legs walk and scissor and scissor. I shoot into my swimming trunks. I feel a significant seep spreading into the towel.

'That was quick,' says Dad, sounding right by my ear.

Fuck. I raise my head, arch my back. But it's okay. He's at the door, not as close as I'd thought.

'You dozed off,' he says. 'Too much sun. I warned you.' I mutter, mutter, mumble something about thinking; I was thinking, I say, that's all. Just thinking.

'Is that a fact,' he says, but not like he's asking. He's giving me one of his looks. He sits down on the step at the door. 'I don't know why you can't admit you dropped off. You're just like your mother.'

Resting my chin onto the backs of my hands, I wonder how I can be like my mother when people usually say I'm just like him. I watch him squinting into the sky. He says he'll have to cut the suckers off the rosebushes at some point. Mum was the rose person before she went back to work. She used to do most of the garden. He says he's not sure if doing the roses is a summer job. He says he's not sure about much in the garden at all. He should read a book about it, he says. Or ask someone who knows.

'Pruning,' I say.

'What?' he says.

I smile. 'The roses. You should be careful, with your back.'

He pulls out his cigarettes, and stares at the box, turning it in his fingers. A glance at me, then he slides it back inside his pocket. 'I wasn't going to,' he says.

I tell him it's none of my business.

I've been quiet, apparently. Absorbed, he says. He notices these things. If there's anything at school, he says I can talk to him. Problems are for sharing. He touches a finger to his chin, rubs a point below his lower lip. He laughs, out of nowhere.

I ask him what he's laughing at.

'The fun I had last Christmas,' he says.

I hate when he says that. Mum says it too sometimes. They must know how much it annoys me. 'Well if you won't tell me,' I say.

'What?' he says. 'If I won't tell you, what?'

I put my head down, shut my eyes.

'Oh, here he comes,' says Dad in a low voice as I'm whiling away in thoughts. Then, 'Afternoon, Jim,' he calls.

It's Jim Willis, the next-door neighbour, out for his afternoon stretch in the garden. He usually sits on his step for a while, his broken flies gaping undone, drinking stewed tea with the bag sodden inside the chipped and stained mug that never gets washed.

'Look at him,' says Willis, nodding towards me as he creaks his carcass across to the low fence. He leans his arms on the top of the fence, holds his swilling mug over our side. His gummy smile is sticky with pink wetness and his eyes wander over me. 'I've seen more meat on a butcher's pencil,' he says, cackling.

I look at Dad and he rolls his eyes at me. I turn away.

I've caught old Willis staring at me a few times this summer and each time it's happened I've lowered my eyelids so he wouldn't know I'd clocked him. I've felt a puzzling thrill as his gaze pulled at my trunks while oldman saliva dribbled from his lips. I don't understand where he fits in with phases and the like. I'm trying to figure it out, and it's his secret, let him have it, and it's my secret that I know, whatever it happens to be. I'm too skinny for myself but not for him, apparently. He seems to like some aspect of what he sees. But he'd be the first to call the men who hang out at the Lisbon in town a bunch of queers. He's not one of them. He had a wife. He still has, I think, although she was removed and put into a care home. But there's kids, and grandkids, stories of all the family, and photos on the mantelpiece. He's safely surrounded by the trappings of convention.

I stare at the broken picket fence on the other side that separates us from Mrs Dodd's place. She's a wizened hunched thing, hundreds of years old, and it's hard to believe her son came out of her body. He's tall, raven-black hair, on the dole, has his own council flat. He rides a motorbike that he fixes up in his mother's back garden. Oily engine parts get spread over the lawn at weekends. His girlfriend looks like another skinny boy. They're always together, in faded jeans and black t-shirts with heavy-metal logos, drinking Coke and bathing in tinny music from the kitchen radio.

Dad comes back to the step. 'Don't worry about him,' he says.

I look up. 'Who?'

He nods towards the Willis side. 'He doesn't know any better.'

'I don't care,' I say.

'He's old. He'll be gone soon,' he says.

'Where's he going?' I say.

'Earlier,' he says, 'I should have put the book down. I didn't realise you wanted to talk.'

I shake my head.

'I got the feeling there was something on your mind, the way you were hanging around,' he says.

'Nothing's on my mind,' I say.

He blows air through his lips in a tuneless whistle. 'I don't know how you can stand it in this sun all day long,' he says. 'Do you need me to do your back again?'

I squirm on the towel. 'I like the sun,' I say.

'Where's the suntan cream?' he says.

'It's lotion. I don't need any now,' I say. 'It's the end of the day.'

'What do you think about all day while you're out here frying yourself?'

I don't answer.

'Maybe you can give me a hand with the roses sometime. We'll ask your mother what needs to be done.' He stands up and stretches his back out. 'It's a heat trap out here,' he says. 'Too sticky.' He pats the pocket with the cigarettes. Then he goes back inside, to his kitchen and his books and those unsmoked cigarettes that nudge at him every time he feels their bump in his pocket. Back to whatever occupies his mind when he's alone.

I turn onto my back. Too sticky. Mr Willis has gone indoors too. He's left his back door open, as usual. He'll be out again later, but not till the light's going, and then he'll begin his nightly watering of his plants. Sometimes he sits out in the dark gazing into the bottom of his garden. Everything round here is always as usual. Nothing happens, nothing changes. It'll be this way forever and ever.

The light turns chartreuse through the leaves as the sun dips lower. Mum will be home soon. She'll drop the evening paper onto the table, and the house will fill with teatime chatter. Tales from the office. How was your day? What's on TV tonight? Before she gets back, I'll get dressed. I don't want her seeing me like this, in swimming trunks. My body occupies a male domain for now. I touch the dampness at the front of my trunks, and allow my fingers to linger, gently probing the fleshiness beneath. Come out, Mr Willis. Have a good look. Let them all look, I think, high on returning desire. I don't care. I'm swelling beneath my fingertips.

***

That night, I sit on the edge of the bed in my underwear, door shut, the only light coming from the dim bulb in my bedside lamp. I smooth fragrant after-sun lotion onto my hot skin. I watch myself in the long mirror on the wardrobe door. In that diffuse light, blurred by atmosphere, I am the paperboy, or Michael or another boy from school, or any boy. The body is another's, the hand on the thigh mine. And like that, he's in the room with me. We're together on the bed. The music is for him. I whisper to him about phases. Let's enjoy this while it lasts, I say. It doesn't define us, it's just a glimpse. I caress the lotion into the tops of my legs, his legs, plunging my fingers into the meagre meat of the upper thighs. The strokes grow longer and longer, and I turn myself on and let my fingers tease inside the underwear. I lie back, tantalised, carried away again.

PLAYFUL ARRANGEMENTS

He's up with the birds, usually. Before them, even. Reeling at the shock of cold water splashes on pasty skin. This is always where the day starts: staring out into the sky, into the depths of dark yard silence. Waiting for light to peel over the edges. In this way, he considers the things done the day before, and how these activities might easily become those for the day ahead. He could visit once again the strangers who live by the bridge. He could stare along the river's reach, towards the lumbering shipyards, and at the fishermen dotting the rocks. Or instead he could sit home, thinking. All alone. Thinking forwards and backwards. Circling around all the things that have to be done, and then all the things that could be done, but in the end not doing any of them.

It was the Sunday of the long weekend. The meatless Friday had come and gone without note. Saturday had been spent down by the bridge. But today he played a song in his room. The same song over and over. 'I'll never tire of this,' but knowing he probably would. Then knowing he definitely will, eventually. Because it usually happens that way. Maybe it'll always happen the same way. Then, a shout from somewhere, to turn the music down. He turned it up. But the shout again, louder this time, and with an edge. He shut the music all the way off. The tune would be remembered outside his room, and the words too. He put on a heavy coat, went out, walked nowhere, walked everywhere, and the tune stayed with him, playing within; the lyrics too, but the words were becoming mixed up. Placed differently, and deliberately, maybe. Twisted to suit himself, maybe. Worked over to fit his own rules of rhyme and rhythm. He enjoyed the playful arrangements he was crafting. This song, a new song, a fluid song, kept him company. The tune stayed the same, he thought.

He walked for hours. Walked in a certain way, without aim or need. Ambled, you might say. Through the greyest of the dreary streets, past rows of small damp houses with smells of stale margarine and old roasts and rubbish, feeling that he was completely safe, that he was alone in the entire place, the only one about in this daylight. Only him on this day, save for bored cats and curious dogs. The light had a dulled-metal cast to it, and he felt as if not just his but all life might go on forever like this; as if this were an eternal light, the light from the end of the world.

And then the solitude was disrupted. By a man, parading outside a ruined pub. The man, unable to walk properly, noticed the territorial intrusion and stopped shuffling. Stood, leaning on a dirty old crutch. Leaning, and peering along the street. Malevolence in the stare. Perhaps.

He slowed then halted at the man's unwavering glare, at the frayed clothes weighted with a history of oily filth. He turned from the man and walked away, retracing, back the way he'd come, picking up the pace. No coward, but sensible. Radar attuned to possible threats. At the end of the street, he checked back over his shoulder. The man had shifted some way from his original position, and was crutching along the pavement. Advancing.

So he ran. He darted round many corners, sometimes into dank narrow alleys, losing himself inside an imagined spiral, and he didn't recognise the place he ended up. Here were houses that looked neglected, even those that weren't abandoned. It was growing dark, and a light mist was falling in patches like fine rain. He hurried along, and came upon a bus stop with a cracked timetable, and sat inside the shelter. The night people would be out soon to claim the streets with painted hair and tight clothes and strange perfumes. Windows were lighting behind closed curtains. The sodium glow from cold street lamps split the vaporous air. A car approached, slowed briefly as it passed, a passenger's face pressed to the window. The music from earlier had left him, without his noticing its departure. He reached for it, but it was beyond him. He knew it would return, as soon as he played the song again, inside his room, and that when it did, the feelings would come back, and especially the feeling that he was invincible. It would all come back.

Home now. It's dark, and the window is propped open. It's cold outside, but he likes to listen to the wind and the tap of the base of the blind against the frame. The door swings lightly, back and forth. The music has gone for the time being, but he doesn't have a need for it. Not right now. He's thinking about the man from earlier in the day. He'll replay the song later. His eyes close. The house is settled. But something is ticking, apart from the blind, slow and even. Ticking, and maybe it'll send him to sleep.

IT WAS CALLED CASSIDY'S

I was at Killen's house again last Friday night. My unit's at the end of the street, and I walk past his place every night after work. That evening, because of the heat, I'd picked up an armful of beers on the way home. The bottles were straining the plastic bag and clunking into my legs. He was out the front, leaning on the gate as he watched over the meagre comings and goings of the street. 'What are you up to?' he said.

'Cooking dinner,' I said, grinning and lifting up the bag, and at first he wasn't sure what I was on about, but when he heard the bottles he laughed. The next thing we were clearing books and blankets off the two old armchairs on his veranda and drinking the first beers warm, waiting for the rest to chill in the freezer. Later, moths batted like crazy into the outdoor lamps, the beer had gone, and we were working our way through a bottle of Scotch he'd found in his kitchen.

He asked me about work, and all its ongoing issues, but I wasn't really in the mood for discussing it or them. Friday was the only night of the weekend when Monday was an eternity away, and I didn't want to talk the next week into my head.

I didn't mind when he began talking about his own jobs from his past. These were familiar stories, and occasionally I'd pick up a fragment of something previously unheard. Like a cherished book, the twists and turns of the plot might be known, but each fresh reading adds depth and a more nuanced understanding to the material.

He's been employed in a variety of jobs in his time. At a service station, for a public service radio broadcaster, in an insurance claims assessor's offices. For two years, a lengthy period for him, he worked in the stockroom of a London department store that he refuses to name. I've wondered if he's concerned that he's spilled too many beans about the store's operations and its eccentric staff members, though what he thinks I might do with the information is beyond me.

Now those jobs are history and he's living on the money his mother left when she died. It's been years since he worked for a regular paycheque. These days he writes music: long rambling folksy songs that he says are mainly for his own enjoyment. He's certain his mother's legacy will have run out by the time he's sixty, and he'll be left to struggle again. He says as he gets older he's become increasingly unemployable, which for him is a good thing because he doesn't want to work, but he senses a crisis is coming and he doesn't know how he'll deal with it.

I'm always careful when Killen's talking not to appear overly interested, or at least not to probe too much. He talks the way he looks, which is tall and rangy, and you have to crane your mind a little to understand what he's saying. And even then it can be a struggle. And you get the feeling that if he catches you peering too closely at what he's telling you, if he suspects that you're taking it too seriously, holding it up to the light and examining it, he might pull it all back inside and clam up. I've learned to keep a distance, to show just enough interest to keep him talking.

That night I made a few observations and asides, light touches to indicate I was following, but I was really away somewhere else, floating in the space on the veranda where nothing mattered. I was lulled by the sense we'd had these conversations before and we'd have them again, and there was no urgency to understand it all.

We meandered into talk of our youthful years. The shape of our conversation confirmed a sensibility in Killen which reassured me, and offered optimistic glimpses of the future of our friendship. He related a few compelling things about his mother, which cast her in an exciting and alternative light. She used to be a fortune teller. I think he'd mentioned that before, but I hadn't realised she did it for money. It was cash in hand, so she kept it quiet. Her neighbours suspected she was a sex worker because of the comings and goings. She uncovered their gossip one day and, though surprised initially, she grew to enjoy the thrilling illusion that had been created around her.

'She's allowed me this glimpse of life without the need to work. I've really appreciated the opportunity. And I know it's not over. Not quite yet. I'm grateful.' He sat forward and peered myopically at the street. It was just smoky light out there and the smell of old heat rising slowly from the baked ground. The neighbours sitting in their living rooms, or side by side in their beds. 'I'll be penniless by middle age,' he said, bringing it back to the veranda.

I didn't point out that we'd both probably be considered middle-aged already. Or that he owns his mother's house, and had done so for some time, and that this was more than a glimpse of life without work. I didn't compare his position to the precariousness of mine. Renting, and bills, nothing saved, and no end in sight. I viewed Killen as fortunate, his situation as idyllic, and secure, and stable. He was being a little insensitive to cast himself in the role that really was mine.

'At least I'm prepared,' he said, 'for old age. Emotionally, I mean. I've been ready for it since I was a boy.' He'd been stubborn and resistant to the early grand designs for him to study, to become a doctor, a lawyer, a scientist. Anything requiring a decent education. 'All that ambition did was repel me, and I've ended up qualified for nothing but this.' He swept a hand around the veranda. His guitar was propped in the corner. I understood his point but would rather he saw the scene on the veranda, which included me, in a more positive light.

I told him about my own mother. I was aware that I might have been repeating stuff he'd already heard, but I wanted him to understand that struggle and difficulty were not his alone. However, my bad memories never seem quite as terrible out loud. Or perhaps I usually end up not quite articulating what I want to say in the way I want to say it. I described how my mother never talked much – that's been an issue for me for a long time, but it always sounds trivial when I verbalise it.

'Some people are distant,' he suggested. 'Private. A little guarded.'

But she wasn't what you'd call distant. 'I learned to smoke from her,' I said, as though she'd sat me down one evening for instruction. 'I've never told her, but when I was younger I picked up her habit of three or four cigarettes every evening after dinner. I watched her some nights, from just inside the screen door. It was hypnotic, the way she stood on the veranda blowing smoke, quiet and still. I wanted that. I started getting my hands on cigarettes, and going for long walks at night along the beach. I'd smoke and look out to sea. It felt so illicit and thrilling. I'd get home late, shower and go straight to bed. She never asked me where I went.'

'That's unusual behaviour for a boy,' he said. 'Is it?'

'Smoking, alone on the beach. How old were you?' His eyes were rheumy. I wondered if he was drunker than I'd thought.

'Thirteen, maybe,' I said. 'Thirteen, fourteen.'

'Didn't you have friends?'

I had to think about this. Friends were never really my thing. 'One or two. I wasn't a good mixer.'

'Lonely Steven,' he said. 'All by himself on the beach. And enough money to buy his own cigarettes. Where'd you get the money for the cigarettes?'

'I had a job,' I said, quickly. 'After school.'

'What did you do?'

'A couple of different jobs. It was a while ago.' I looked at the table, at the liquor bottle. 'A bar was one of them.'

He smiled. 'A bar? That's pretty young to be working in a bar. There are laws against that kind of thing.'

'It was more like a cafe. A licensed cafe. Anyway, fourteen's not so young. I washed the dishes. Back of house activities. The rules were different then.' I was warming to my story, so I spun it out as best I could. 'I did two afternoons a week,' I said, details suddenly coming easily. 'It was a casual arrangement. The owner was a friend of my mother. It wasn't a formal job. More a favour. You know the kind of thing. To help him out. But the money came in handy.'

'What was the place called?'

I hesitated. 'It's a long time ago. Why do you ask?'

'I'm interested. It doesn't matter, if you can't remember.' All I could see was Bob Cassidy pressing money into my damp hand at night on the beach. 'Cassidy's,' I said. 'It was called Cassidy's, after the owner.'

He nodded. The brown flecks in his eyes had become familiar to me; I'd studied them, as an artist about to paint a portrait might, but sometimes felt as if I were falling into a deep and inescapable chasm. I had to close my eyes to shut it off.

'Okay?' he said.

'Fine. Relaxed, maybe.'

'Call it a night?' he said.

'I'll never be the first to call it a night,' I said. 'Some nights,' I said, thinking back, 'I didn't feel like walking at the beach, so I'd stand outside with her. On the veranda. I thought she might offer me one of her cigarettes. She never did. I asked her once, how did it taste? She blew smoke into my face and smiled.'

'She knew what you were up to,' he said. 'From the smell. On your clothes and breath.'

'I don't think so. I was careful,' I said. 'I only smoked outdoors. There are ways.'

He laughed. 'If you say so. But it's not just the smell. Of course she knew,' he said. 'Mothers know these things. It's their business.'

I didn't share his ideas. I'm certain she didn't know. I was there, he wasn't.

A sudden awkward quiet rained over us. It's easy for offence to occur between people, and I'm not sure who'd offended whom, but something had started between us.

'Tell me some more about your mother,' he said, softening the mood by settling right back into the old stuffed chair.

I pictured her, as if she were with us right there on Killen's yellow-lit veranda. That unusual way she had, and may still have, of smoking with her elbow resting on the other forearm, the cigarette held away from her head. The smoke curling away from her hair. Distant nights, in a faraway place. So long ago, it seems. It's comforting to know I could return there if I wanted to. To that place of my youth, to that beach, if I needed to. It still exists, forever. I could sit, just like I used to, and though I don't smoke anymore, I'd start up again for old time's sake and gaze out to the careless sea.

Killen's phone rang from inside the house, interrupting. He jumped up to answer. But it kept on going with its jerky melody while he stomped about on the floorboards, cursing and looking all over the place for it.

I helped myself to more Scotch, and slouched and stretched my legs to the edge of the veranda. Killen's murmuring phone voice drifted to me from a room off the hallway. The boozy lull and the warm night combined to a soothing balm. I closed my eyes on the restless creatures shifting about in the garden, and floated away and back to that distant beach where I grew up.

My nights on the beach, homework and dinner all finished with, my mother at home doing whatever it was she did when I wasn't around. Her mysteries, and my mysteries, and the two never meeting. Those nights were the making of the finished form of me. My ideas about where to go, and what to do, crystallised there, even if they hadn't been realised. Back then, I looked away to the edge of the sea, the line where the earth went round the bend and disappeared, and conjured what existed beyond. I'd look in the direction of the city – never visible, but I knew it as a place – and I'd feel the electric pull of its demimonde of spangled streets and kinky people. I'd fantasise about grinding my cigarette into the sand, walking to the road, and hitching a ride in one of the cars that occasionally passed through the centre of our home town.

***

A car stops ahead of me. I walk up to it, a little unsure. The driver leans over to open the passenger door. 'Climb in,' he says. He is good-looking, and speaks softly. He waits while I settle into the seat. I shift so I can observe his profile without having to turn my head too obviously. He checks that everything's okay, asks me where I'm headed. The city, I say. We begin the drive. There is a lengthy and straight stretch of road out of town, and we start to talk out the monotony. The radio is low, tuned to a talk station; there's a muted scent of layered cologne from the upholstery; the man is a fast, confident driver, and his face is firm and angular in the dashboard lights. Dark shapes come and go outside the car, and the radio soundtracks our slight conversation and smooths down the sharp edges from the things we tell each other.

I know – and this is hard for me to accept because it represents a missed opportunity, one that I'm too old to grab now, and was too cowardly to grab then – that nights and journeys such as this exist. Meetings like this happen every day in towns all over the world. Young men climb into the warm dark cars of strangers, and find the radio tuned to tinny music or late talk, and sit back as the road and the hours stretch ahead. The lives of these boys will change, and not always for the better, but there will be a shift. They'll find out what happens when they take a risk. But though I took some risks, I ended up sticking it out in that town till I was an adult. And when I finally left, it was on a train.

***

'That was Jay,' said Killen, pushing his phone into the side pocket of his jeans.

I don't know a Jay, but I nodded and pulled myself back from the roads of my youth.

'Were you sleeping?' he said, narrowing his eyes.

I shook my head, and said I'd been thinking.

'Oh yes,' he said. 'Thinking.' He said it the way my mother used to say it when she disturbed me in the middle of a daytime nap, drawing the words out as if pretending to be fooled. It annoyed me now, as it used to annoy me with her.

He stretched up to the roof over the veranda and arched his back. Where his shirt split open at the top of his jeans I glimpsed the body of a man much younger, smooth and taut and new like fresh milk. Here was someone who cared about their appearance. He yawned, lowered his arms and looked at me, as if to say, 'Well, what do you think?' Probably my imagination wilding into fantasies. I continued to admire his lower body; felt brazen staring down into those forbidden areas, but I found him so compelling that I didn't want to tear my gaze away.

We'd kissed, one night, some time ago. Months earlier. His mouth had tasted of warm copper or blood, and its tissues were alive with hot energy. The event, and to me it was an event, worthy of remark, had never been properly discussed since it occurred. At the time, we'd both been so sodden in booze that it was

difficult to pinpoint exactly how the physical contact had come about. There must have been an initiator. Every event has one, I suppose. After the kiss, he took off his glasses and wiped them on his shirt, and smiled and told me that I was confusing him. This led me to believe I'd opened a door for him, that the confusion was brought about by desires and drives that he didn't understand and had never had to confront or deal with before. And I took from this an implied understanding that we might continue to explore each other. But the situation didn't develop further, and since that day I've wondered if his confusion might simply have been about me. Perhaps the kiss had been a complete surprise, and had shown him a side of me he hadn't been at all aware of, and that the confusion he'd mentioned had been regarding my supposedly sending out mixed signals.

I know about an ex-girlfriend of his, Suzanne, from a rambling recollection, made confusing by my over analysing parts of it at the time of the telling, thereby missing the subsequent parts. I didn't really understand what was underlying the story, and the details are gone from my mind now. It had no point for me, other than to let me know that this Suzanne, this female figure from his past, still occupied his thoughts from time to time. Finally, when I'd been trying to make sense of it, wondering how to respond, he'd said that these days he prefers the company of men. 'Really?' I'd said, trying to keep my eyes from widening. 'Oh, men are much more straightforward,' he'd said.

I thought about this conversation later. At times I saw promising signs in what he'd said; but the promise could very easily turn to flat simplicity on closer inspection. However, I kept coming back to his preferring the company of men, and saw in 'these days' a turning away from a previous self.

Now, I can't fit the events into a line: I don't know if the Suzanne story came before the kiss. And I can't tell you how long we kissed for. It was a deep kiss but it could have lasted for ten minutes or two, or less. And in trying to recall the kiss in such detail, and fearing that my memory of it might dull over time, I've even begun to have a slight doubt that it happened at all.

He shivered. 'It's chilly,' he said, but I wasn't feeling it. He sniffed, picked up the bottle and held it to the veranda lamp. 'I'll make some coffee.' He went inside.

His words contained a quiet signal for the beginning of the end of the night, perhaps. Perhaps I was over thinking, as usual. It was Friday night, or maybe Saturday morning at that stage, and I had no work till Monday, and Killen didn't work at anything anymore except endlessly picking apart and reassembling fragments of his own songs.

I would have liked the coffee to arrive in steaming mugs laced with more whisky, and for it to be a prelude to the next stage of the night. Killen's house is close to a river, and I entertained the thought that later on we might take a leisurely walk down there and watch the still moonlit water before stripping off and diving in. I wanted this for all its accompaniments: the fleshy contact in the freezing water, the shivering banter on the riverbank, and the boisterous rush back to the house for hot showers and scalding coffee.

I hadn't been night-swimming since my teenaged summers. That was how I first encountered Bob Cassidy at the beach. Usually the beach would be deserted on those nights, but this one time I came out of the water, head down and watching for broken shells and sharp stones, and I looked up to see Bob standing right by my neatly layered pile of clothing. I was startled at first because I didn't recognise him. He said it was dangerous to swim on your own, especially at night with no one else around. I told him he was around. He laughed. I asked him if he had a dog. 'Are you walking your dog?'

I said. 'No,' he said. 'No dog.' He was often there after that, making sure I was okay when I swam. Sometimes we'd sit on the sand and I'd smoke while he watched me. And we'd talk, and it felt as if I could say anything to him. And because he was an adult, whatever I said to him was okay, as long as he didn't say otherwise. And he never said otherwise. I spoke freer in front of him than I'd ever spoken, even with school friends. It was something to do with the dark, and the surf-noise, and the smoking, maybe. I told him how I really felt about things, peppering my language with fucks and cunts, and he never pulled me up for any of it. He gave the best advice, because he didn't give any advice, apart from telling me not to swim alone at night, and that was right at the start. He just listened. Then one night, I told him about my plans to go to the city. I described the whole fantasy: the car, the man, the radio and the cologne.

***

A rustle from the bushes at the base of the veranda. Rats scrabbling round, or a bird or a frog. It came again and I pulled my feet beneath the chair. I wondered, have I reached an endpoint in my life? For years, I dreamed of living in a large city, finally arrived, and it spat me out the other side. Living there was like being inside the drum of a washing machine.

Killen came out wiping his hands on his jeans. The sweet smell of jasmine soap, and his face scrubbed, and he'd pulled on a sweatshirt. His hair was dampened and swept behind his ears. His face suited pallid tiredness. He glanced at the bottle.

I told him how my mother's one-liners could be so spot-on that sometimes I'd laugh for ages while she smiled wisely, but then I'd see her later the same day with eyes faraway and reddened, and I'd wonder what had happened to her in the meantime. I often try to recall an instance of this, a detail to bring it to life. But I can't quite grasp it. I wonder what in the world we found to talk about in all the years I was living with her. We shared a living space, but maybe not much else. Certainly not our confidences. We moved through the house like an old and rather unhappily married couple talking in non sequiturs, which is worse than arguing. We led completely separate lives. It's how I wanted it at the time but now I wonder if she was disappointed with the hand she'd been dealt.

But Killen looked at me as if he didn't know why I was telling him any of this, as if he'd lost the join in the conversation. He was quiet for a long time. I wanted to ask him about the phone call, about Jay, and tried to think of clever ways to do it. But the possibilities felt clumsy, sounding to my internal ear as if I might be grabbing for something. I didn't want him to think me needy. I sighed and considered just asking him what the fuck was wrong with him tonight. Why he'd turned so moody.

He said, 'You could always ask her.'

'Ask her what?' I said.

'Your mother. Ask her what it was like.'

I shook my head. 'They're not the conversations we have in my family. We don't hold things up to the light.'

He closed his eyes. I studied his face and allowed my thoughts to retreat to the time of those night swims, and smoking, and the newness of my body. Such a recent time in so many ways. Yet, at times like this, so distant.

Bats were screeching from the treetops. I envied them their uncomplicated life. Killen brought out a French press and two chipped china cups on a beaten tin tray. He put the tray down next to the Scotch. I poured us chasers for the coffee. There was no milk on the tray. 'You've forgotten the milk,' I said. 'There is no milk,' he said. My face was taut from the things on my mind. Killen was smiling. He was amused, and I fancied he was looking at me the way one might gaze at a lover. Tenderly, perhaps. It was just the whisky or my imagination or a fusion of the two. Anyway, there's no reason to be anxious with one who's tender, whose mouth is soft and coppery, who has clumsily forgotten to stock his fridge with milk for the week.

THIS IS THE TIME

A recent episode: We're wagging school. Cut grass and birdsong, and Slyder's tongue tasting of his morning fix, smoky and dark. I'm holding him as he gets hard. But when the woman passes with the kid in the pram, he says, 'What the fuck are you staring at?' and she speeds off. It was puzzling, and not like him. The woman was just curious. I walked away, telling him I'd see him later. He kept his distance. A few nights forward, I went round to his place, half-cut on cheap sherry. His mother, guarding the gate, told me to go home. 'Sleep it off, love,' she said. But I must have sweet-talked my way inside. Slyder was at his keyboard, working. He took me to the park. We sat on the swings. I leaned my head on the chain. I was feeling sorry for myself. I said he was his mother's dog. That he licks her feet, and his mouth tastes of her salt and the shit and ash from where she stands in the front yard. 'Your breath stinks of it,' I said. He just sat there, swinging and staring at the ground. When I apologised, he said it was fine, that it was strong lyrical material.

***

Friday: I go over to Slyder's place after school. His mother's out the front, sitting on the old orange milk crate, intimidating the neighbours. She's smoking Benson & Hedges and her amber coffee mug is at her feet. She flicks me a look and makes me walk round the back. Slyder was in bed, sheets pulled up to his chin. I haven't seen him around all week. He's been busy with the new track. His keyboards and headphones were spread over the floor in scribbles of wires. He looked like shit. Waxy skin, feverred lips, and oil-darkened hair. That familiar sour smell. But the track's finished. It emerged from his nightmare of thousands of birds sheltering under a bridge, screaming in terror at an approaching calamity. I tell him I don't want to hear the track. I've heard earlier iterations, and it puts something inside me I don't like. I scan the room. I want to ask him if Jack's been round. I push hair from his damp brow. He tells me to fuck off, but holds back the sheet. I look at the door. 'Don't worry about her,' he says. I keep my clothes on, the way he likes it. He comes quickly, like he's been saving it up, then says he has to sleep. I pass his mother creeping about in the hallway.

***

Those screaming birds might be us, sensing an approach or recognising a departure.

***

Sunday: Jack throws another private party in his flat above Terminus. He's closed the bar for the night. I'm capturing video for Slyder's music. Everyone's wearing a mask. In a corner, a horse in underwear and stilettos describes a melancholic fantasy. 'You're an unusual invitee,' he says. 'I'm just here for the pictures,' I tell him.

***

Later at the party, Jack cryptically cautions me to exercise good judgement. 'I'm not only talking about your film,' he says, and he gestures dismissively at my phone. 'You and Slyder may be the threat that people cross the street to avoid,' he says, echoing a line of Slyder's lyrics, 'but crossing streets isn't something I do.' He insists on seeing the film I've captured before I upload or share it.

***

Jack's through everything now, like the colouring in a cake. I tell Slyder it was better when it was just the two of us, making music and fucking around with videos and pictures. 'But the money,' he says. 'The connections.' Yeah, the benevolent showerings of an old man. For all Slyder's smarts, he's pretty naive.

***

Tonight: I took a series of torch-lit pictures at the disused meat-canning works. Slyder naked, scrawny, shivering, aroused. I got all I needed, and he reluctantly got dressed. He'd wanted me to jerk him off, but I'm starting to take back some control.

***

We sat on the wall near the river landing. I offered him my phone to view the raw images, but he said he'll wait till they're ready to publish. My latest images are hyper-edited. I crop, apply filters, rotate, until his beautiful cock is manipulated into coded abstractions. His foreskin becomes a nipple; his balls a peach bleached of colour. He likes the way the tiniest details of his body are public. His aunt Julie has shown some of these to her bingo friends and her latest squeeze. She says the pictures remind her of alien landscapes. 'If she only knew,' says Slyder, 'she'd be frigging herself off over it.'

***

I take another picture: Our legs touching; my hand resting on his thigh, fingers edging the bulge in his jeans. You can see the wall in the space between his thighs. We're washed by brash yellow neon from the path lighting. Sodium glare cuts through the vaporous night. This is the time: just me and him and the river-smell, and no terms or conditions.

SO MUCH LEMONADE

The boy sat on a shady patch of grass at the side of the car. His sister was seated in the car. He watched his parents unload bags and containers and a blanket from the boot. He turned to look towards the edge of the cliffs, and out beyond where the far rim of the horizon dazzled and shimmered. Seagulls hovered, swirling and unbothered by the unseen drop from land to sand.

'Did we remember the napkins?' said the boy's father.

'Is she going to sit in the car all afternoon?' said his mother.

'She can sit if she wants,' said the father, low-voiced and kindly, with a glance towards the girl.

'She's sulking.' His mother soured her face, like a clown. 'Are you sulking? Like a little baby?'

'I'm not sulking,' said his sister from the car. She was addressing the mother but looking at the boy, so the tenderness of her expression didn't match the acid in her voice. 'I'm tired. Tired and bored,' she said.

The boy studied her face. Her hair hung just short of her shoulders; her nose, though she often described it as stubby, was neat and petite.

His father spread the rug onto the patch of grass behind the car. He stood back, lifted a corner, pulled it tighter, and put his fist on his hip. 'Which way's the sun?' he said. The sky was as bright as a clean towel, the shoreline hidden but audible, the sea unmoving at the shimmering horizon.

'There must be toilets here somewhere,' his mother said, scanning along the edge of the cliffs in both directions.

'I saw some when we drove onto the grass back there,' said his father.

The mother frowned, a plastic lid in her hand, surprised at receiving a response. She turned away, shielded her eyes from the sun. 'I'll wait till after lunch,' she said.

The car door was open. The sister had shifted herself in the seat, so that one of her bare feet was on the grass. She was wriggling her toes in the cool green blades. Her skirt had ridden higher, so that her upper thighs were exposed, milky and smooth. She had an unlit cigarette in one hand, a lighter in the other, and she seemed as far away as the horizon.

She noticed him staring, and gathered her expression. 'Let's go for a walk,' she said, low and kindly like their father earlier. Her eyes were bluer than the sea, and just as resigned. 'We'll take our time. And maybe we won't come back.'

She laughed. 'If only it were just you and me,' she said, leaning in to him. 'Things would be much easier.' She slid out of the car, smoothed her skirt over her thighs, and grabbed his hand. 'I'm taking him for a walk,' she said over her shoulder.

'He's not a dog,' said his mother.

'We'll be just over there,' said his sister, pointing towards the sea.

'No, stay away from the edge,' said the father.

His sister laughed and pulled him close and squeezed his hand.

'We're about to eat,' said the mother. 'Wait till we've had lunch.'

'Bloody hell,' said his sister, but the words got lost in the wind before the parents could catch them. She hesitated as if she might be considering the walk anyway, but then, still holding hands, they went back to the car.

***

On the way to the picnic area, they'd stopped at a service station. The father had wanted to get some coffee. He got out of the car, and shoved the keys into his pocket. 'I won't be long,' he'd said.

'I'll come with you,' the girl said. 'I could do with a smoke.'

'You might as well turn off the radio,' said the mother. 'I'm not listening.'

'Are you sure you don't want anything?' said the father. The mother pulled a face. 'Nothing for me,' she replied, looking straight ahead, out of the windscreen. 'I'll wait till we get there. It can't be much further now. It hardly seems worth stopping.'

'I need a coffee. A stretch of the legs.'

'Come on, Dad,' the girl called.

The father leaned in to switch the radio off. The door was closed with a thud. Then it was just the boy and his mother. The air inside the car was hot, and it made him sleepy. He looked at his mother in the passenger seat. She put her head back and closed her eyes. He wished his sister had taken him with her. He also closed his eyes.

When he woke, his mother was asleep, her head turned to the side. He'd never watched her sleeping before, and her lolling head with its open mouth and closed eyes made him frightened.

He turned to the window. His father and sister were walking towards the car. He didn't look at his mother again until the car door was open, and his sister was saying, 'Been sleeping, Mum?'

The mother ignored her. His father started the car. They carried on with the drive in silence. It didn't take long to arrive. His father had said you could tell when you were near to the sea. 'Look how the sky seems to get bigger,' he'd said. No one had replied.

***

The father picked up the rug, faced towards the edge of the cliffs, and shook the rug out then replaced it further from the car. He kept fiddling with the corners, lifting, replacing, smoothing.

'Stop fussing,' said the mother.

The father's back stiffened, but he carried on.

'After lunch,' his sister said to the boy, 'we'll go for a long stroll.' She angled her face towards the parents, but held the boy's gaze and raised her volume. 'Yes. A long, long stroll. We'll walk till we get too tired to carry on, and then we'll sleep where we fall, keep each other warm, then wake with the dawn birds, start again, and keep going.'

'Stop being so ridiculous,' said the mother.

The father had moved the rug again, and was carefully laying plates and cutlery onto it.

His sister held her expression, and continued. 'We'll find our way, without any help. Me and you.' She picked up the boy and sat him on the bonnet of the car so they were almost at eye level. She put her hand on her hip, just like their father had done earlier. Then she lit her cigarette. Blowing smoke away from the boy, she said, loudly, 'I could sell my body. I reckon we'd get by.' She winked.

'Lunch is served,' said the father. 'And you can get your own child,' he said, lifting the boy off the bonnet.

'I don't want my own,' she said, self-assured with her cigarette and short skirt and so-blue eyes.

'Then what do you want this one for?' he said, holding the boy close to his chest. He smelled of Old Spice and the softness of warm wood. He kissed the boy on the forehead.

'Company,' she said, crinkling her eyes at the boy then staring at the father. 'Someone to share my troubles with.'

'What troubles?' said his father.

'Just troubles. Anyway, he always listens to me.' She flicked ash from her cigarette.

'I'm sorry to disillusion you, but he's going to keep me company in my old age. Aren't you?' said the father.

Wrapped in Old Spice, strong arms, salt-sweet skin, the boy was content with this design for his life.

His sister laughed. 'Lucky Dad,' she said.

The father gave the daughter a rueful look, as if there were nothing lucky at all about him.

'Am I to eat alone?' said the mother.

His father took the boy across and sat him on the rug. He tickled him in an armpit, and the boy giggled and rolled over.

'Be careful,' the mother said. 'Don't upset the picnic things.' She shook her head.

The sister sat on the rug, and carried on, taunting: 'I can see it now, as clear as that car.' Apart from the boy, they all looked at the car, as if some part of the girl's thoughts would appear on its shellacked surface. 'We'll move far away, me and him. Somewhere new, somewhere warmer. Naples, or Casablanca. Byron Bay, perhaps.'

'Byron Bay?' said the mother. 'I don't know why you waste your breath on fantasy. And put that out. I can't eat with the smell.'

The girl ignored her, and stared away to the edge of the cliffs. The father spooned potato salad onto the plates, and added thin slices of boiled ham, beetroot and white bread.

The girl threw her cigarette away. The mother told her to get up and put the cigarette out. 'Do you want to be responsible for setting the grass alight?'

The father started to tell them about how he used to come here as a boy. 'It was exactly the same as you see it now. I always looked forward to visiting. As an adult too. We often drove here before we were married.' He turned towards his wife. 'And then after we were married.' He put his plate down. 'We stopped coming,' he said. 'I suppose we couldn't find the time. And now it's nice to be able to visit the place again.' He looked at the boy. 'When did we last come here?' said the father to the mother. 'Can you remember?'

'Is it important?' said the mother.

'A question with a question, Mum,' said the girl.

'No,' said the father. 'It doesn't really matter.' He looked at his daughter. 'Can you remember when we were last here? You would have been close to your brother's age.'

'I remember coming here,' said the sister. 'But I couldn't tell you when it was.' She smiled. 'I remember something, though.'

'What?' said the father.

'Well, I remember arriving here on a beautiful sunny day. A day like today. But it was a much warmer day. We started to unpack the picnic things. It was very quiet, just like it is now.'

'And you can remember all that?' he said.

'Now that you've asked me about it, yes. I remember.'

'She's going to say something funny,' said the mother. 'What do you mean?' said the daughter. 'What do you mean, Mum?'

'I can tell. You're going to pull us along with this, and then you'll throw a surprise into the middle of your story.'

'What's she talking about, Dad?' said the girl.

'Just carry on with your story,' he said.

'I don't want to now,' she said, folding her arms.

'Don't stop on my account,' said the mother.

The girl pouted, as if she were finished with something. 'Carry on,' said the father.

'I don't want to,' she said. 'It's not really a story. I was just going to say that I remember being here, and the weather. And you were wearing shorts, Dad.' She laughed. 'Yes! You were wearing shorts. Maybe we can date it from that?'

The father laughed. 'It's been a while since I've worn shorts,' he said.

'It's best that grown men stay away from shorts,' said the mother.

'I always thought you looked good in your shorts,' said the daughter.

'Boys wear shorts,' said the mother. 'Not men.'

'Why did you stop wearing shorts, Dad?'

The father said nothing.

The girl looked straight at her mother and smiled wickedly. 'Did you like Dad wearing shorts, Mum?'

'Men shouldn't wear shorts,' she said. 'My father never wore shorts. That's how I knew he was a man. He was my father, not my younger brother.'

'Dad,' said the daughter, 'why did you stop wearing shorts?'

'I don't know,' said the father.

'You don't know?'

'I just stopped.'

'You stopped? No reason?'

'Do we always need reasons?' said the mother.

'Can't you let him speak?'

'I am here, you know,' said the father.

'Then tell us,' said the daughter.

'You're showing us up in public,' said the mother.

'But there's no one else here, Mum. Not for miles and miles.'

The boy looked around. They were the only people in sight. The buildings near to the road were like toys. They wobbled as he stared. In the other direction, the sea. If the ground were sloping, they might all start to roll along the grass, building up speed until they reached the edge. And then they'd fall down and down onto the beach below.

'We're the only ones here,' his sister said. 'I could scream, and no one would hear me.'

'We'd hear you, unfortunately,' said the mother.

'I feel like screaming sometimes. I feel like screaming at the top of my voice, until my throat hurts.'

'Don't be silly,' said the mother.

The father was watching the daughter closely.

'Well, I do. Sometimes I feel like screaming.'

***

After they'd eaten, his mother stood like a sentinel and took in the scenery. His father began to clear the wares from the rug, whistling in his tuneless way.

'I might want some more later,' said the mother. Everything was replaced onto the rug.

His sister lit another cigarette and stretched her legs out. She smoked and appraised her feet, turning them at the ankle. The boy also looked at her feet. Her toenails were painted green. She noticed him looking and reached out to him, the way he'd tried earlier with a ladybird on his mother's arm. His sister encircled him in her ivory arms.

'Are you warm?' she said. He nodded. She clamped her cigarette between her teeth, and took off each of his shoes, then the socks. His feet felt softened from the sea air. She put her nose to one of them, looking at him all the time. 'Little boys,' she said, 'smell so scrumptious. I could eat you up!'

The boy moved pieces of food around on his plate, trying to arrange them into a satisfying shape.

'I think he might become an artist,' said his sister. Her underwear was visible where the skirt had risen. 'A painter, maybe.'

'Careful, and blow that smoke away,' said the mother. She looked nervous, as if an invasion from the sea were imminent, and was wringing her fingers over and over.

'Or a writer,' said the girl. 'He'll write poetry or a novel, and make us all very proud.'

His father seemed to find this idea agreeable. 'A writer,' he said, shielding his eyes and looking towards the sea.

'And what about you?' said the mother, freezing the girl with a dead stare. 'How are you going to make us all proud?'

'Aren't you proud already?' she said.

'Would you be?' said the mother. 'If you were me, would you be proud?'

'Come on,' said the father, as if he were about to announce something. Everyone turned to look. Perhaps he never intended anything; if he did, he'd changed his mind. Either way, all he said was, 'Anyone for any more?' This was one of his phrases. No one answered him.

The boy hadn't finished his cup of lemonade. He picked it up and peered inside. A small fly was swimming at the surface. He touched his finger to the liquid, and the fly swam to it and clung on to his skin. He pulled his finger out, looked at the drowning fly and then wiped it on his skinny tanned leg. They were all watching him.

'I need to piss,' said the girl.

'Pauline!' said her father.

'Your mouth!' said her mother.

'It's all that lemonade,' she said, standing and wincing. 'So much lemonade. We really know how to have a good time.' She looked to the cliffs again. There was a group of seagulls near the edge, squawking and swooping around. One of them was standing still, apart, facing all the others. The boy followed the noise and her gaze.

'Listen to me,' said the mother, slow and pointed. 'I'd like you to watch how you speak.' She cocked her head towards the boy.

But the girl had become absorbed by the birds. 'It must be so easy,' she said, 'being a bird.

Just flying, looking for food, sleeping. The occasional fight over scraps of food, perhaps. And bothersome humans getting in the way sometimes.'

The boy wondered how his sister knew all this about seagulls. His mother said, 'Don't be ridiculous. You're not a bird, you're an adult. It's time you started taking things seriously.'

'Oh I do,' said the girl. 'I take things very seriously, Mum.' She was looking right at her mother when she said this, and the mother seemed perturbed by the stare or the blue of the eyes, and quickly glanced away. 'I'll be back,' said the girl. She stood and brushed crumbs from her skirt and began to hum a familiar tune. The boy watched her go. He let the paper plate drop onto the rug.

The mother took the opportunity to light a cigarette. She crossed her arms and watched for the girl returning.

The seagulls had flown away. The boy walked to where the birds had been standing, but all that was left was a single feather. He looked back to his parents. The mother was gazing dreamily to wherever the wisps of smoke took her. The father was beginning to tidy away some of the bits and pieces of their picnic; when they left, later that afternoon, there would be no trace of them ever having been there.

The feather fluttered on the ground. He reached towards it. As he did, the wind gusted harder, and blew the feather over the edge of the cliff. It floated on the air, level with the boy's head. And then it was snatched away sharply by the wind and carried far out.

The sea below the cliff rolled, white on blue, and broke on the sand. He watched the waves, and the patterns and colours within the body of water. He felt a curious draw towards the water, its swellings and undulations mesmeric.

He moved closer to the edge: a beautiful sheer drop, like something had been sliced off the land; just salty air and colour. Hovering above it all, like strokes of brilliant white oil paint, enjoying the life that his sister had described, was the flock of seagulls they'd watched earlier.

He caught some wind in his hands, and wavered from side to side. He heard his mother say, 'Oh Christ.'

'Don't call out,' his father said.

The boy smelled his father before he saw or felt him. And then he was lifted swiftly and firmly into the air, as if by the seaside winds.

***

His father carried him to the car, put him inside and shut the doors. The boy stared out of the window, and wondered where his sister had gone. It was warm inside the car, and he fell asleep, and when he woke again, they were driving along the road. The radio was off, and it was dark outside. His sister was filing a nail on her left hand. He watched her closely. She had a strange expression on her face, as if her mind wasn't on her hand or the nail or her filing. His father suddenly said, 'Nearly there.' The boy looked at the back of his father's seat, then moved his head slightly to see his father's hand steady on the gearstick. His mother's head was resting back on her seat, and she might have been asleep again, but it was difficult to tell. He looked at his sister, and she peeped out from beneath her fringe, and smiled a small smile, sweet and a little sad, so that it wasn't like a smile at all. Then his father said, 'Yes, we're nearly there. About ten or fifteen minutes more, I'd say. It's always good to get home, isn't it?' But no one replied.

CAREERING

The appointment started off well enough. The careers officer seemed to take a quick shine to me. He asked me to sit down, then closed the door, and he took a long time to return to his desk, and I fancied he might be checking me out from behind my chair. I liked the calm of his office. An official smell, of paper and files and biro ink. The man had an odd kind of a smile that never completely left his face. I'd missed his name at the beginning, when I walked in and he offered his hand, but it didn't seem important so I didn't ask him to repeat it. He told me that I was his last of the day. 'Last what?' I asked. I knew he meant the appointment, but I was in a light-hearted mood. He offered me a confidential aside on the slowness and tedium of the afternoon's earlier interviews. I wondered if he used the same routine on everyone, but I smiled back, to please him, and to make him believe I was flattered, that I was falling for his patter, and to make the time in the office as smooth and easy as I could.

He opened a manila folder. He peered at me. 'Michael,' he said.

'Mike,' I corrected.

He said he'd been looking over my file, coming to his point in his practised way, 'and you seem to be a very capable student.' He asked if I'd given any thought to what I might do when I left school later that year. I nodded. He nodded too. Then he asked me to picture the environment I'd like to work in. He told me to take my time, and when I was ready I was to tell him all about it.

I looked around his office. It was the room, I supposed, where he spent most of his time in the day, and therefore most of the time in his life. The side wall had a row of gunmetal filing cabinets. There was an old-fashioned hatstand in the corner by the window holding a man's coat and umbrella, and another coat, perhaps from the woman at the desk outside.

I began to describe a small office in an old dilapidated building in a corner of the town centre that people rarely visit. Inside are echoey, dimly lit corridors. Just four of us work in the office, including Fullerton, the branch manager. Margaret is a dedicated smoker, and the place is filled with her smoke by ten every morning. George is also a smoker, but he smokes less and prefers to go outside for his cigarettes. The paint on the cold stone walls has become yellowed with nicotine. It's worse towards the ceiling. Even the paperwork in the filing cabinets smells of old smoke. The phones only ring about four, five times a day. Sometimes we let them ring and ring and don't bother to pick up. There are other businesses in the building, but we only have a vague idea of what they are, or who works there. We rarely see the other workers from these offices, but we might pass in the corridors, say hello, how are you, off anywhere nice tonight? That sort of thing. There's a shared bathroom near the top of the stairs. You need a key to get in, so that people can't come in off the street to use it. It's always freezing in there, because the slatted window above the toilet is broken, and cold air has been rushing through for years. The light in the bathroom flickers on and off occasionally. The tap water is like ice, so cold it peels the skin from your hands in winter. On the edge of the sink there's an old piece of soap that's cracked and discoloured but has a nice clean scent. The office is a decent place to work. It suits me. It's slipped under the radar in many ways, and head office isn't really aware of its operations, or doesn't care any longer. We don't make waves, and we get left alone. The workload is light and easy, and predictable. Everything follows a weekly routine. It's reassuring. There's no chance of promotion, because the only senior position is the manager's role, and Fullerton will be there till he curls up and dies, because he knows as well as the rest of us that we're onto a good thing in that place. No one cares for the idea of promotion anyway. Fullerton's not on that much more money, as far as we know, and he sometimes has to stay late or come in on weekends. The staff remains the same year in and year out. Just the four of us, like I said. We go for drinks at the Eagle round the corner on special occasions. Birthdays, Fridays. Christmas, obviously. At Christmas, we buy each other gifts. Just tokens. Chocolates, fragrance, talc, accessories. Stuff like that. Margaret sometimes gets drunk on rum and blackcurrant when we go out on Fridays, and when she does she swears like a docker after she's back at her desk. One time, Fullerton calls her into his office. They are in there a while, and when she comes out she says she's going home early. Neither me nor George mention anything when she comes in the next week. I have notebooks in a desk drawer which I keep locked, and I take the key whenever I leave the office. I spend the quiet parts of the days, and sometimes my breaks, or the evenings when everyone else has gone home, filling the books with poetry. The poetry will never be seen by another human being. That's the reason I write it. Because the minute I think someone else might read it, it's become too self-aware. Except the cleaner catches me writing in the books a few times, and he asks me about the poetry. I put my finger to my lips, tell him it's a secret, not to tell anyone. Then I show him a few pages of what I've written. Just this once I make an exception. I watch his face closely as he reads, and when he's finished we look at each other for a long time, and all the while outside is the sound of traffic and gangs of kids shouting from the empty market stalls just below the window.

The room creaked, like it was shifting out of a cramp. For a moment I wasn't sure where I was. I blinked a few times. The careers officer came back into focus. He was frowning and slowly massaging his temples. He closed the folder and squared it with his desk. His fingernails were neat, trimmed and clean. Pink and healthy. I wondered what his fingers smelled like. 'Yes,' he said, staring at the folder. He looked up. 'Thank you, Mike. Yes, that's very interesting. Is there anything you'd like to add?'

I thought for a second. 'Mr Fullerton,' I said.

'I beg your pardon?'

'The manager, Mr Fullerton. One day he asks me if he can have a quiet word, and he takes me into his office. He closes the door. We sit opposite each other, in swivel chairs. He says I've been working there a few years now. He asks me to call him Roger. Sure, I say. He asks if I'd like something to drink. Sure, I say again. He grabs a bottle from one of the drawers in the filing cabinet, and two mugs, and he pours some of the drink into each mug. He hands one to me. Thanks, Mr Fullerton, I say. Roger, he says. I sniff at the mug. It's whisky. Oh yes, I say. Roger. I forgot. Then Fullerton, or Roger, he starts telling me in this really low voice about his wife and his two children and the disjointed lives they all lead in a quiet street in a quiet neighbourhood where everything's turned to stone. He pauses every so often, and checks the door, or looks at me, and when he does this I nod to show I'm listening. It's like he's waiting for stuff to sink in, but I wonder if he's been on the sauce in secret at lunchtime. Then he wheels his chair closer to mine. You like to write poetry, don't you? he says. Yes, I say. He goes quiet. I cough. He puts his hand on my knee. Lets it rest there. He says that he feels life is slipping by, faster and faster, and he wants to stop it all from disappearing. He says he used to enjoy reading poetry, at school, but other things got in the way. He says it's all going too quickly for him, that it's difficult to cope. He asks me if I'm also finding life too speedy. I don't say anything to this because I'm not sure if I am or if I'm not. He says that maybe we could become friends. His fingers flex very gently on my knee. I ask him what he means, even though I know what he means. He tells me that if we became friends, and saw a little of each other outside work, then maybe I could read some of my poetry to him.'

The careers officer looked up at the clock then down to his wristwatch. He said we'd almost run out of time. 'I think we'd better leave it there,' he said. He stood and thanked me for coming in to see him, even though I'd really had no choice in the matter. He came round the desk, put a hand on my shoulder then withdrew it quickly. He walked to the door of his office, and held it open for me to leave. I smiled at the receptionist, but she looked past me to where the careers officer was probably still standing.

I walked out of the school grounds, over the main road, through the car park, past the cinema, and towards the shops. I bought a bag of hot chips and sat on a bench to eat them. I did some thinking about the interview, rerunning it in my head. I didn't eat all the chips – I wasn't as hungry as I'd thought. I wrapped what was left and put it into my backpack to have later, cold. I smoked some cigarettes and thought some more about the interview. People came and went. It started to get dark.

HOT SPELL

The rusty car rattles west, along the highway that bisects the derelict industrial sites before dipping down to the shipyards. On either side of the road, shells of buildings crouch, shrouded in climbing weeds and decades of graffiti. The evening is thick: windless and lazy, the sun at first hanging full and ripe, an orange orb over the docks, then falling away as they reach the bridge, so that floodlights in the yards pick out high wire fences enclosing gigantic machines shifting shipping containers in a graceful choreography.

Traffic is sparse on the bridge and the coast road, and they find a sedate and steady pace. Ahead lies the settling still of the twilit landscape, its vague edges suggestive and tantalising with promise.

Ted's shirtsleeves are rolled and cuffed to reveal tanned hairy forearms; a lock of fringe falls into his eyes; he needs a shave. He taps the air conditioner. It's still on the blink, he says. Best keep your window lowered for some breeze.

Steven winds his all the way down, puts his head towards the air and closes his eyes. The radio: that works. That's always worked. Now it's playing old-time ballads, no commercials, interrupted only for information about the music. The presenter's voice when it comes is low and cakey, and the combination of this, the mellow residue of the day's heat, and the storied melodies, lulls Steven into an easy sleep.

He dreams: of unpeopled airy rooms in a large crumbling house billowing with natural light and soft breezes. These are rooms he's never seen before, though they're familiar in some primal way, like a gut feeling, so that he's able to move through the house with the calm of one who anticipates the terrain well, without effort or rush, confident of not meeting another person, marvelling at the touch of a soft fabric here, the dusty floral scent of a long-closed drawer there. It's a long dream, uneventful. All he does is move through the house.

When he wakes, blinking at the sudden departure from the dreamscape, it's with the sense of something having been revealed. But he can't put a finger on it.

The car is bumping over a loose surface, and light and colour have drained from the sky and been replaced with the cloak of night. The radio has been turned off.

Ted glances over, sits up straighter in the driver's seat. 'You were well away,' he says. He taps a finger on the steering wheel, like a nervous tic. He says the diner isn't much further now, that they're on the approach road.

Steven checks his wristwatch against the dashboard clock. He was sleeping for almost forty minutes. He stretches his neck out, flexes his leg muscles against the floor of the car. He feels like he's woken up in the wrong part of the sleep cycle, and his head is fuzzed. He asks if Ted's sure that Angela's Diner is still going.

Ted smiles. That might have been a more pertinent question to ask before they'd set off, he suggests. He's right, of course. Despite the smile, his face is sombre in the glow from the dash. There's a look he carries these days. Not older so much as wiser, more resigned, knowing. He says he's visited the diner a few times recently. It's much the same now as it always was. Except for the crowd; yes, the crowd is different. The last time he'd gone was a few weeks ago. He'd been driving around to take his mind away, and in trying to get lost he'd become hungry and sought dinner somewhere along a nostalgic turn in the road.

'A long way to go for something to eat,' says Steven, thinking more of Ted's attempting to get lost, and bookmarking it for a future conversation.

Before long, Angela's is lifting from the dark on the left, its brutal sprawl covering the coastal rocks, high above the fomenting surf. Garish, its lights; a guide for shipping, they used to say, and of note even from space. And beyond this neon skyline, and far out in the middle of the sea, its outline just visible, is the brooding presence of the unnamed island made uninhabitable after a spate of industrial accidents in the early seventies.

The car moves slowly, crunching over gravel and broken glass, through the forest of illuminated signposts at the roadsides. The signs advertise pie and coffee, fresh seafood, air-conditioned dining rooms. One, 'WE NEVER CLOSE', is the largest, and its confident constancy has, he recalls, always been a source of comfort to Steven.

Frying oils, appetising at this time of night, lace the air. Cars are pulled over, doors wide, bodies and music spilling out to the roadside. Folding chairs here and there. Blankets, towels. Cheap wine casks, six-packs, soft drink bottles. Packets of crisps, biscuits, cigarettes.

Through the car windows waft tobacco and cannabis smoke, pockets of stale coconut suntan lotions and chemist's perfumes and cheap spray deodorants mixing with dried sweat. And over this adolescent beach fug, the sulphurous coastline strikes a fierce note at the back of the nose. Steven wondered once if that smell was natural, from the sea, or toxic spew from the factories hiding round the curve in the bay. Either way the smell has never been unpleasant for him, but evocative, taking him back to coming to Angela's Diner for the first time, behind his parents' backs, fifteen and scared with excitement, a whispered illicit world finally within his grasp.

Ted pulls up to the entrance, and turns off the engine. They sit for a while in the confines. The engine ticks as it breathes. The drive has taken just short of an hour and a half. As teenagers it had never seemed that far. In those days they'd come with their girlfriends, friendly foursomes, Steven and Ted trying out straight masculine roles, convincingly they thought, guessing at and assuming expected sexual positions while longing, unknown to each other at the time, for the hard angular sensations of other boys' bodies. Then later, in the summers between college terms, they'd continued to visit Angela's, this time with the truth laid out between them. No longer afraid to name and discuss their desires, they egged each other on in sexual adventure. They played guessing games in those days, wondering which of the schoolboys they watched twining in the limbs of girlfriends were as reluctant as they themselves had once been. It became their usual game, this, and one tinged with an element of wishful thinking. To their freshly opened eyes, homoerotic signifiers were everywhere. Each glance, smile, word, gesture, was open for interpretation. It was a time of thrilling possibilities.

The old days. But 'old days', it's just a turn of phrase. Isn't it? These memories, they're fairly recent still, and not so old, not yet. Not so distant, surely. And yet.

Ted gets out of the car. Steven watches him stretch, notes the youthfulness his friend's body has retained over the years, how it belies the cast of the accompanying face.

Steven also gets out. Sniffs the air, looks over to the island. Hears the bell, that bell, clanging still from some dark and lonely place out at sea. It's always been there. Right now its single intermittent note is clear, but has been at times in the past muffled, occasionally less regular, sometimes drifting or lost on the wind. Its source is a puzzle, and now, years later, he's no closer to understanding or wanting to understand the mystery.

'Coming?'

He follows Ted into the dining room. The interior is brighter and noisier and cluttered with more fittings than Steven remembers. Here are the tattered red booths, fabric ripped and interrupted with crude patches; and over there the beaten metal service counter. The same chipped dusty models of fat-loaded burgers and foaming milkshakes adorn the walls. The old plastic-laminate tables, scratched and scored with graffiti, remain laden with grubby sauce bottles and salt dispensers. And above the door is the manic blue ceramic fish that will hang forever askew and grinning. The air is choked with smoky oil and vinegar and the sweetness of soda and cheap ice-cream.

The line is short. While they wait, Steven looks at the menu board above the counter without really reading it. He knows what he's going to have. The items are printed in black on a white background, and he's fairly sure they'd once been red on white. He can't be certain. It doesn't matter, he knows, though the detail seems significant, to him anyway, and he considers asking Ted, out of interest, but knows that Ted won't appreciate his wanting to recall the detail, and will have no idea about the menu's colour scheme, and will be reluctant to entertain the memory, will take the enquiry as an indication that Steven is once again obsessing over irrelevancies.

The server reads their order back, says it won't be long, and passes a numbered receipt to Ted, who gives it to Steven. 'I'm off to the toilet,' he says, and Steven resists a pathetic urge to ask him to wait till the food's arrived.

A cleaner is outside the unisex toilet, given up fighting the endless battle with wrappers and scraps littering the floor. He swipes an ungloved hand across the screen of his phone. Ted brushes past him and disappears inside.

The light in the dining room is stark, the crowd noisy, the overall effect one of hostility, so that the easiest of tasks is suddenly beyond Steven: he's unsure what to do with his hands, where to put them, how to hold his body. He wants at least to look confident and is sure he appears anything but. He's probably twice the age of most of the other people in the room, yet everybody else looks more at ease. Surely at this age he should be inhabiting a more placid space. He breathes deep to steady himself, and there's a hint of noxious stomach gas in the air.

He looks around. So much activity. Too much. His eyeballs feel as if they're moving very quickly from side to side, and he rubs them briefly to end the sensation. In the nearest booth just by the counter is a group of five, late teens to early twenties. They're squashed close together on the narrow benches. Two boys are kissing rapaciously, eyes closed, mouths sucking and licking at each other's lips. They break apart, then one puts food into the mouth of the other, and the devouring resumes. A third goes through the items on a long list, possibly a receipt, checking and marking the paper with a pen. Another, impossibly thin, body and features possessing a seamless fluidity of razor hardness and fine delicacy, applies nail polish while a phone is held to their ear by the fifth member of the group. Steven makes an effort not to overhear any snatches of the phone conversation; he's sure an occasional word gleaned here or there will only generate more questions than answers. The kissers are especially fascinating for their unselfconscious blurring of conventional lines with their very public display of arousal. He catches himself staring and looks away, aware that his attentions could be construed as inappropriately prurient, should anyone care. And he cares; he doesn't want to be a person who can now only derive pleasure from observing that of others. Remaining a player matters to him.

Ted comes back, wet hair pushed behind his ears, splashes at the front of his shirt. He gives Steven a look, up and down, like he's making sure this is the same person. 'The toilets are in a right state,' he says.

Steven nods. What can he say? He wants to get outside, to feel fresh air upon his face. Their order number is called out by the server. Steven hands the ticket over. Two plastic trays are slid across the counter.

The uniformed guard at the door says sorry, trays not allowed outside. There's not enough staff to retrieve items. More: he says that the cleaners have refused to do it, because it's not within their remit. He goes further: there have been complaints, he says, from locals, concerning debris on the beach and clifftop. Steven nods. He sees Ted suppressing a grin. They slide their trays into the vertical racks provided, and the man holds the door open for them to pass with their food.

'I didn't think there were any residents around here,' says Steven outside.

'You tend to have a rather searching expression. He probably realised you're the type who always needs reasons,' says Ted. And before Steven can probe, Ted moves ahead.

They make their way to an unlit treeless area back from the edge of the rocks. The few benches are either broken or filthy or occupied, so they take a space on the ground. To the left, a couple of teenagers also sit on the ground, united in embrace. Their bodies are bloodless and sculptured, statues caught in moonlight. He's in short swimming trunks, hair long and straight with an oily gleam. He's leaning back into her arms, so they're both facing the same way. They watch Steven and Ted settle, and neither attempts to avert their gaze. The boy whispers up to her, lazy, slow. She smiles down at him. She catches Steven's gaze, and though her smile holds steady, the look in her eyes wavers, betraying a note of uncertainty. Hers is an expression tinged with anxiety, somewhat wary, as if she is alert to potential threats at all times. She moves her head closer to the boy's, rests her chin onto his shoulder, watches Steven.

Steven unwraps his burger. It's soggy, limp. He turns it, examines it, then rewraps it. He pokes around in the pocket of fries, eats, sucks salt and grease from his fingertips, and wipes his fingers with a napkin.

He wonders whether he or Ted ever looked as self-assured as the boy nearby. He wants to go over, to take the boy's hand, tell him that aloofness is a waste of time, that they're all going to end up the same way, their futures ultimately shared. Imagining the soft hand, cool and slightly damp inside his own, fills him with a powerful yearning, but he struggles to see a way that this might be satisfied here. The distance to his desired result is too great, involves much manoeuvring and many machinations – he doesn't have the energy for any of it. He lies back and stretches his long body out.

'You not eating the burger?' says Ted.

'Maybe. Later,' he says, irked at the brashness of Ted's appetite. 'I'll eat it cold,' he says. He watches Ted chewing, draining the last of his milkshake.

Ted covers his mouth as he belches quietly. He stands and stretches his back. 'I won't be long,' he says, moving towards the trees.

Steven wonders if Ted's idea of 'long' will turn out to have the same loose meaning now as it usually did when they were younger. While his friend is gone he amuses himself by looking for shapes and patterns in the stars, and trying to make sense of the moon, gauging its distance, searching for the elusive man in its surface, and falling into the reassuring kind of stupor that can come with the unconstrained contemplation of the cosmos.

Around him, people come and go, but he's stopped looking at them. He hears them, smells them, senses their movements. There's gentle laughter, haunting music. None of it troubles him. The sky is soothing. It's hard to tell what is nearby, what far. And the inevitable tolling of that distant bell. He can pick out its note if he concentrates. He waits for the next metallic sounding, tries to locate its position. It comes and it's all around, of the air, so that any pinpointing of a source is impossible. It hails from the sea, it comes from inland; from near, from far. It's easy to believe the bell might be tolling from the skies.

Much later Steven senses Ted's return. Steven can tell it's him, without even looking. This presence of a being that he'll have to interact with fractures his serenity. After a while, he sits up. 'Where did you go?' he says, trying to sound casual.

'Here and there,' says Ted. He's hugging his legs, looking seaward.

Two shirtless men saunter by, full of themselves, a tangle of smooth skin and limbs. One turns to look over his shoulder, then turns back. Whether the glance was meant for Steven or Ted it was hard to tell, but there had been a calculating awareness in the eyes. A direct look, it seemed to hint at invitation.

A chance! thinks Steven. Action is all that's ever required in such situations. He knows well how it works. He just has to get up now and follow the men at a discreet distance. No one will judge him. Ted would urge him on. He'll wait for one of the men to turn around and notice him and realise what he's up to. A locking of eyes. That should be more than enough to confirm an interest. No words would be necessary. A contract signed. Intentions acknowledged. The men will pause then smile and wait for him to catch up. The three will move to the steps, go down to the beach. They'll find a quiet spot, remove their clothes and touch, all three, no talking. As the activity progresses, it will turn out that one of them is more into it than the other. Things work out that way sometimes, but that's okay. The imagined scenario promises an easy execution, is easy to draw on, and so vivid he's surprised to find that he's actually still sitting on the ground next to Ted. Maybe he's been up in the stars too long.

Ted has been watching him. 'I don't think you'd be interested in what they're into,' he says.

'How do you know?' says Steven.

'We've known each other a long time, you and I. I've a pretty solid idea of what you're into.'

'I meant those two.'

'We became acquainted,' says Ted, 'just now.' He licks his lips in what's meant to be a comical show of salaciousness. His eyes, however, are full of mischief and dark vapour, and Steven wonders if he's shared a drug with the men.

'Oh,' says Steven. He's irked, not for the first time, by Ted's ability to find satisfaction so easily. Ted has always managed to encounter opportunity all around, in any situation. Maybe he's more willing than Steven to settle for whatever's on offer. Either way, Steven's beginning to feel excluded from the sexual playground surrounding them. 'Which one?' he asks.

'Both.'

His insides slip a notch with the thought of missed opportunities.

'You think too much,' says Ted. 'Go,' he says. 'Go and explore. I'll be fine here. Find a diversion.'

But Steven doesn't move. He's no longer sure he knows or even cares what shape diversion takes in this environment. 'How often do you come here?' he asks.

'Occasionally. It's too far. Petrol's expensive.' The weak smile again. 'I never asked you before now because ... well, Eric. I was never sure how it was with you two. You always seemed so caught up. Happy families and all. It was so wholesome, your set-up. And this place is. Well.'

Well. Caught up, maybe. But happy? That's an unrecognisable description. Ted refers to wholesomeness as if it were an affliction. Maybe it is. And that family, happy or otherwise, is ended now. Steven puts his head back and stares again into the suspension of stars. He has the sensation he often experiences in wide open spaces, in meadows or on beaches, that gravity could fail, or might be switched off, that he'd then fall from the face of the earth and hurtle into the infinite skies.

Caught up. Perhaps that's always been his way. He locates images within the stars, of lattices shaped like nets, of traps, contraptions, and he thinks of immersion. A memory arrives from the time of his eighteenth birthday: just him and Yvonne. Yvonne had driven the car to Angela's so they could celebrate together. They'd parked and moved through the charade of fumbling kisses and gropes in the front of the car. They'd been bickering all evening. Trifling disagreements, about not enough attention being paid, about misunderstood or misheard statements. They took a booth at the diner. The night suddenly seemed to yawn ahead, vast and tiring. The atmosphere became taut. They argued, over this and that, the food, the future, but nothing worthy of remembering. He got up and walked out, leaving Yvonne in the booth by herself. Outside, he turned to see her through the glass but she wasn't looking in his direction. He walked away from the diner. He was expecting her to follow, all remorse and apology, the way she usually did. But this time she stayed inside.

He walked with no idea or care for a destination. He ended up a long way from the diner, the grey sea for company. A gloomy setting. Threatening in a way, but strangely reassuring in its solitude. He wanted to remain forever, to become stone like the rest of the world. He would lose his inconvenient desires, and never have to return to the rolling challenges of the day-to-day.

He stayed out all night. In a funk, unaware of the passing of time. He had no concern for getting home. The sun crept up and threw silver off the water. He sensed a closing presence behind him. The air had chilled. He turned, and blooms of blue mist were moving towards the rocks. He stood and followed their trail. The mists spilled, over the edge, down to the beach, like ghost vapours of liquid nitrogen.

His father had talked about blue mists on that section of coast. The phenomenon had been, he'd said, responsible for shipwrecks, unsolved disappearances, sudden madnesses. 'Evil blue zephyrs,' he'd called them. An unusual word choice, it may have been a combination of his father's basic English and a love of old European folk tales. A clumsy attempt at deterring Steven from visiting Angela's. His parents, in common with many of their generation, thought the diner a lover's lane of moral ruin. The blue mists were possibly a version of the bogeyman.

But Steven had never been afraid of bogeymen. He'd scrambled down the steep descent, stumbling several times on loose rocks. At the bottom, he sat on the firm sand, in the clammy cool of the blue haze. His eyes closed, he was aware only of sensation, and of sound, the shushing of the waves and of the hollow ghostly clanging of a faraway bell.

When he'd opened his eyes, the sun had burned off the mists, or they'd rolled out further, to sea, or simply dissipated. There was one other person on the beach that morning. An older man, his father's generation, but nothing like his father. The man was slim and fit and dressed for swimming. His belongings had been placed in a neat grouping at the shoreline.

These days Steven wonders often about Yvonne, and the man at the beach. Yvonne might well be married now. There could be kids. Does she ever remember Steven, allow him to occupy her thoughts in this way? If she recalls him at all, is it as a strange boy from a turbulent time, a fleeting recollection of an experience that she puts down to the vicissitudes of puberty? And the swimmer, the man from the beach? Patient, gentle, understanding, guiding. Why did Steven not attempt to see him again? As soon as it was over, as soon as he'd been satisfied, all Steven wanted was to get away, quickly, to clean himself up and get off the beach. He hadn't returned the favour, hadn't yet learned the etiquette of sexual reciprocation. And the man, who'd once been a callow youth himself, had probably understood. A benefit of experience, that. The man had watched from the shore as Steven scrambled up the rocks. Thank you, Steven had called, cringing later on at the ghastly ineptness of the comment. And then, at the top, he stood, panting, feeling vaguely uneasy as suddenly the noise of the bell seemed much closer. And then the sound was fainter than ever, whipped away and carried elsewhere by the wind. He caught his breath again. He realised he had no means of getting home.

'Coming for a walk?' Ted's voice, rousing, brings him back. Ted springs to his feet, holds out a hand, pulls Steven up and keeps the hand pressed at Steven's back as they weave between people on the ground, making their way to the edge.

The sky is wide and gusty. The island hulks in the distance. A sound comes from below like a loud crack. Someone shrieks, then laughter, and shapes jerking about in the surf. 'Skinny-dippers,' says Ted.

'That bell,' says Steven, squinting as if that might clarify the now faint sound.

'The bell buoy?' says Ted.

Steven's mind at first constructs 'bell boy', then 'bellboy'. And he thinks that his friend might be making another joke, about service staff at the diner. Later, he will discover that Ted was referring to the nautical device. But now he nods, not wanting to show he has no idea what Ted's on about.

'What of it?' says Ted.

He shakes his head. 'Nothing.'

'Come on, it's too windy here.'

Inside the trees a few metres back from the rocks, small groups of people sit in loose circles. Incense and weed perfume the air. Someone is humming a simple repetitive melody in a minor key. Ted moves further in. Steven follows. The wind drops. Dried twigs crackle underfoot. Branches pull on their clothing. Ted stops and turns and places his hand on the back of Steven's head. He guides their faces together. Their mouths meet. They've been friends for a long time, but this is the first time they've kissed. Steven keeps his eyes open. Ted's tongue is all iron and salt and lemon from the fish. It's a comforting, pleasing taste, a hark back to schooldays. But a scent lies beneath, the residue of a dirty musky cologne. All Steven can think about is this mouth's liaisons with the men from earlier on. You wouldn't like what they're into. He pulls away, and leaves Ted and heads off, out of the trees, not caring if his friend's following or not.

They emerge from the scrub onto the edge of the car park near the main road. The street lamps show a wasteland of wild grass, plastic bags, tyres, cigarette packets, condoms, cans and bottles and food packaging. Even though it's early, traffic is already roaring heavy in both directions.

Ted moves on, head lowered. He stops to toe at an object on the ground. He bends to pick it up, blows dust off it, looks at it closely then throws it down. 'Your old man's blue mists: they're a natural effect. In hot weather, dust lifts in the wind and mixes with oils from the sea grasses, and it refracts the morning light. The haze is basic physics.' He kicks a burger container, then kicks it again. 'A trick of the light.' Steven doesn't reply. 'Your dad always did have a head for the fanciful. You too. It must be in your genes.'

They walk on. The air tastes of petrol. They arrive back at the car and sit on the edge of the bonnet. The breeze strokes their faces. The sun climbs slow and confident of its place. This has the makings of another baking day, just as the radio man promised the night before. People are leaving, chased by the harsh morning light. Car doors thud, engines rev, the noise of surf and crying gulls mingles with shouts and laughter. Steven wonders how many of those leaving now will still be connected in a year's or a month's time, or even at the end of the next week.

'What are we doing?' says Steven. 'We make a bed, mess it up, remake it. Buy bread, fruit, veg, consume it before it decays. We buy more. Relentless cycles. Rising and setting suns. We're maintaining, that's all. One day becomes another. A week finishes, another starts, and sometimes you don't even notice the days toppling.' He rubs an eye with his index finger. 'Fuck, I'm tired. I haven't slept properly in ages. I'll need to find another job soon. The night work at the factory has dried up. I'll get by for a few months. I'm worrying about the same things as ten, fifteen years ago. Money mainly. What kind of way is this to live? Did I ever tell you work makes me anxious? The pointlessness scares me. I know what you'd say. The point is it pays bills, rent, puts food in the fridge. Keeps the wolf from the door. But repel one wolf and there's always another waiting round the corner.'

Ted has been watching him all the while he's been talking.

'Don't take any notice of me. It's the tiredness talking. A good night's sleep, that usually fixes a gloomy outlook. That's right, isn't it?' He considers Ted's face, tries to size up the expression. Is it a wry look at his lips? There's a hint of something else. Bemusement? No. Amusement, maybe. There's certainly an element of having already seen and heard not just this but everything Steven says or can say. Of expectations refined over time and now always being met just so. Some might call this jaded or faded. But it's more a readiness. Resignation. He wonders if he can ever again say anything that will surprise Ted.

And it's an interesting face, Ted's. Handsome. Always has been. More intense now. Mature, yet vibrant still. For now. What would it be like, Steven wonders, to wake next to that face now they're both well into adulthood? To see it over dinner every night. To be its observer as it advances into its later ages, lining, sagging, mottling and thinning. To hold it between the palms of his hands, and kiss its eyes, the lips, the nose. To watch its expression change during sexual release. That would be something new. He can still taste Ted's lips. These thoughts begin to arouse him, but he doesn't want that. Inconvenient. He pushes them away, looks out to sea. The island is brown and dulled, like it's dead and rotting. And the bell, again, lonely and distant. 'That bell,' he says, to himself more than anything.

'It's reminding us,' says Ted.

A car pulls up nearby. The handbrake is applied with a noisy ratcheting. A family gets out, one by one. Four of them, and then a fifth, right at the end, a small child. The child finds his legs and runs from the others towards the diner. 'Come back,' says the man, but half-heartedly, knowing from experience that the child will be fine, and the child runs on. An older boy, a teenager, says it's all tawdry. 'What's tawdry?' says the man. 'This place,' says the boy. 'Stop spoiling,' says the man. The boy's lip curls. He swears. 'Here we go again,' says the woman. 'Every day's like this,' she says. 'We haven't even had breakfast yet. Why do we bother coming to these places if all you're going to do is row?' They follow the small child over to the diner.

'Fools,' says Ted. About the family, or the two of them, it's difficult to tell. But before Steven can ask him, he says, 'Let's go and face the cycles, as you like to call it.' But they don't go anywhere. They continue to sit, looking out. They've had too much of everything, perhaps, and there is nothing left to rush towards.

The family is swallowed by the restaurant. The roadside signs are right: this place will never close. Steven won't be back again, though. It's too far from where he is now. For that reason, he feels he should take a final look around, the way you might walk through a house you're leaving just before locking the door and handing over the keys, knowing you'll never see the place again. But Angela's is more than the physical diner, and there would be too much to assimilate, and it won't look or be the same in daylight anyway. And he feels tired. He feels old, and is sure that were he to have a mirror to hand, years would have suddenly appeared on his face in the space of the previous night. He wants someone he's never met before to appear and touch his arm and whisper assurances in his ear. But that won't happen. He listens again, carefully and for the final time, to that bell calling from its home; he tries to commit the sound to memory. He's almost ready to leave, and is waiting for Ted to lead the way.

FRAGRANT

He is exuberance, exhilaration, light and sweet violin music. He is the frisson of surprise in a stranger's glance. He is sex in the park in the middle of the day. A bursting run through a meadow of wildflowers. He's the seizing of opportunity. A nudge towards the unknown because if it feels right then what's the worst that can happen? He's a loosening in the heart, a falling away of constraints, a kiss in the margins. He's the allure of night-time, unclothed, lights blazing, curtains open, uncaring. He's not quite the absence of fear and worry and needless concerns, but he's the striving for it. Fuck it, is always his answer. Fuck it.

He rarely sleeps. Time's not for wasting. He wants to feel everything. And when it's dark and still and very late, he leaves the house, goes out in trunks tight and short so the edge of his tattoo is visible. He wears a dab of Patou's Joy at the backs of his knees so the perfume lifts as he walks. Scent can release a story wordlessly, he says. You might see him, if you're ever about in that place at that time: contained, striding, floral; and if you do you'll think nothing or you'll think well that's fine because it fits.

He walks, in his trunks, tattooed and fragrant, down to the bridge, off the river path where the lights don't reach. He writes graffiti, greets the night fishers, engages with the insomniacs, the artists, the disaffected, etcetera. The talk, though usually minimal, dissolves barriers. There's touching, sometimes, and sometimes kissing and more. What does it mean, this? some ask, and if he says anything he tells them it's without meaning, outside it, does everything have to mean something?, it's just the moment.

And to any disapprovers, or head shakers, to those disgusteds of here there and everywhere, he'd say it won't be long till they're dead, all of them. The bridge people, the day people, everybody. All gone forever, into dust, and kindnesses and love will be all that ever mattered.

Do you ever get scared? I asked him once, thinking of the dangers at the bridge at night. He laughed and pulled me closer as if I'm the one who might be afraid. He might be right. I waited for him to answer my question. He didn't, not directly, instead telling me about a party he'd been at recently.

He rarely, if ever, goes to parties.

But he'd somehow ended up at this one, he said. At this party he managed to meet someone he was comfortable talking with. You're funny, she said about the things he was saying. The two of them laughed and talked some more and got a little silly. And then later on, when they were both a bit drunk, she said, let's leave without saying goodbye to anyone. And they did, and when they'd left and were strolling together, outside, she dared him. Go on, she said: take it all off right here in the street. And he did, of course. He needs little encouragement. He's always game. She liked this abandon, his crashing through the barriers of received decency. They arranged to meet the following day. They went to see a Belgian avant-garde film that people are tutting about, and which is probably going to end up being banned. Then drinks afterwards and then a light meal in an elegant place. They discussed the film, both getting into it and both getting high on the conversation. He said out of the blue, let's find a hotel, book into a room, just for kicks, fuck the cost. But aren't you...? she said, trailing off. Into men? he said, finishing politely for her. She nodded. Yes, mostly, he said. He hates labels – I could have told her that. Does anyone do this in real life? she said to him later when they were in the room they'd paid for. They do now, he said. What a buzz! she said. It's just like we're in a movie. And it was, he told me. Intense, but the novelty wore off, as so often happens with intensity, so they called it a day after less than an hour. It was fun while it lasted, though, wasn't it? they agreed. Then they shook hands, friends, laughed, kissed on the cheek. Yes it was really good fun. He told me that it was funny how, after all those fluids, the tastes of their bodies on each other's lips, they'd kissed so demurely at the end. Then he was quiet and that was the sum of his response to my initial question about fear.

So that's him. There's more to tell, but that's all I have to say.

There's a good chance you've seen him yourself. At the end of a night, when you're drunk and hungry and it's a takeaway and a bar of Dairy Milk on the train home. He's the smile in the eyes you'll miss if you aren't paying attention. Or the one you see, but you look away because it's strange when strangers engage. But it stays with you, the smile, because it was luminous, and when you're off the train you wish you'd smiled in return. But it's too late, with that one anyway, so you store up the glow and you make a special effort with the next person who takes your fancy, and it's someone eating sweets at the night bus stop two days later. You check them out, watch them closely. Study them. They might come over and belt you, but you risk it anyway. At first they look away, but then their eyes are back at you, intrigued, curious. And then it's up to you.

When I saw him that first time, our first encounter, he smiled, I smiled back. This wasn't at the bridge, but a train station. There was such light in his expression, and that perfume with its undefined promise. He beckoned. I wanted to follow. But I've got to ... I said, fumbling for an excuse, suddenly cautious. Got to what? he said. There's nothing more important than this. Love and life. Let yourself go, he said, and he touched my arm softly and I spun with wonder and he took me. No, that's not quite right. We went. Together. We went down stairs, into a long subway, curved roof, dirty tiles, years old, around a corner, then another corner, so many turns and hollow unpeopled spaces, then more stairs. He led me someplace that over time and successive meetings became our place, as if it existed only for us. Tunnels and stairways. Dripping water and decades of dust and dirt and oily yellow light. Rats scratching and guttural rumblings from the trains.

That first time. Me and him. I'm glad I went.

BROKEN RULES

My mother threw her last party while I was still in primary school, during the summer of my turning ten. My memories of her from those days are blood-red and fragrant: flashes of lipstick, the whiff of lightly perfumed hair, her drink in one hand and cigarette in the other. Her parties were never big or particularly fancy. She used to tell my father, who didn't care much for parties, that she was just having a few friends over for drinks in the evening. Low-key, she'd call it.

She kept a number of large tumblers stored at the back of a kitchen cupboard, and she liked to polish them in the afternoon before a party. I'd help her as soon as I arrived home from school. We'd place the tumblers into rows on the kitchen counter, and she'd boil a kettle on the cooker, and keep it boiling while we held the glasses inside the clouds of steam, before drying them to a polish with clean cotton tea towels. She told me it mattered how drinks were served, and that the glasses should look and smell spotless. She held a polished tumbler towards my face, and the scent of the laundered fabric of the tea towel came to me from the surface of the warm glass.

Afterwards, she'd fix herself a swift afternoon cocktail, and a smaller version for me. This was always vodka-based, usually paired with a sweetish mixer such as lemonade or orange juice. The first time she did this, she didn't put any liquor in mine; she pretended, but I'd been watching, and I told her I wanted the same drink she was having, and from then on she would always stir a splash of vodka into my drink. I became fond of the way the charged liquid warmed my chest and lent the surfaces of my teeth a rough unfamiliar texture.

The evening of the final party, I'd been throwing a ball outside; catching it, enjoying the thump as it hit the wall over and over. When the light had begun to turn soggy and grey, I went back inside. My mother and her friends were in the room adjacent to the living room. My mother called this room the parlour. She was perched on an arm at one end of the couch, laughing gently, her head thrown back exposing her throat and beads, and thick hair coiling recklessly over those stone-pale shoulders. Beside her were Otto and James, the two welded so you couldn't fathom where one ended and the other began. A woman I recognised from another occasion but whose name I couldn't recall was at the radiogram behind them, reading the liner notes on a record sleeve and moving her head out of time to the music. My mother noticed me. She touched Otto's arm. He shifted, and they indicated the space between them. I joined them on the couch.

Otto smiled and brought his head to mine. 'He gets more handsome every time,' he said, winking at my mother. 'A heartbreaker,' he said. 'Mine's splintering already.' He lifted a glass from the coffee table and offered some of his wine. I took the glass, said thanks, and they laughed. I smiled uncertainly, wary of their amusement. Otto put his arm over my shoulder, in the same way his other arm was around James. 'My two favourites,' he said. 'What a lucky man I am.'

'You're like a cat with the cream,' said my mother. 'Well I'm not sure of that,' he said. He turned to James and removed the cigarette from the corner of his mouth.

'Hey!' said James.

He placed his finger to James's lips, but James shook his head away. Undeterred, Otto took James's chin and manoeuvred the face to kiss its mouth, and in so doing he twisted his body round and withdrew his arm from my shoulders, allowing his hand to fall onto my leg. I watched the men, the subtle movements beneath the skin of their jaws. I was nervous and thrilled, as if caught inside a rolling storm cloud; uncaring of anything else in that room.

And when I look back, I still wonder how it was possible that life progressed elsewhere for the duration of that exquisite event.

The men pulled apart. Otto sat back. James exhaled through lips that were lazy and damp. Otto turned to me. 'Well now, Steven,' he said, 'how about you?' His hand was gone from my leg. I could smell the wine on his breath. The beard of light stubble, skin the shade of jarred honey, and mouth bruised with vigour. His lips, so recently attached to James, were parted slightly, offering a glimpse of a dark interior glisten. He narrowed his eyes, as if by concentration alone he might be able to read me. I caught my breath. Time and the music paused. Only Otto and I existed.

I couldn't hold his stare, and I blinked and looked down. And when I met his eyes again he was smiling faintly. He laughed. 'Don't look so alarmed!' he said.

My mother shifted at my side. She had crossed her legs and was arranging the folds of her dress around the upper knee.

'What troubles could possibly touch a boy like you?' said Otto. He removed a fresh cigarette from the packet. He took his time with the lighting, inhaled deliberately and with satisfaction, then sat back again, watching me through the folds of smoke. Then he held the cigarette out towards me. He nodded.

I turned to my mother for guidance. But she said nothing, searched my face, smiled. She seemed engrossed, as if in a stage performance.

I gingerly took the cigarette from Otto's fingers. It jumped and flicked to life in my own.

He took it back from me. 'Watch,' he said. He held it carefully between two fingers, pouted and then brought it to his lips and pulled his breath through the filter. 'It's easy,' he said, exhaling smoke, passing the cigarette back.

I sized up the cigarette, then tried to copy him, but I wasn't able to contain the smoke inside my mouth for long. I spluttered, and the adults laughed, even usually surly James. This time my mother put an arm round me, her face next to mine. Small blisters of sweat beaded at her upper lip, and her lipstick was patchy close up. She asked if I was okay. Her hair, violet-black and with the delicate scent of newly fallen apples, tickled at my cheek.

I told her I was fine, because I wanted to be fine. But the smoke in the room was stinging my eyes, and I said this in a whisper so the men wouldn't hear. She pushed loose strands of hair from my forehead. She offered her drink, but I shook my head.

I slid off the couch and stood at the doorway. I walked down the hall to visit my father in his study. He opened his arms when I came in, and I went over and leaned into his thigh. He put down his pen and took off his glasses and grabbed the sides of my face in his dry warm hands, and kissed the top of my hair.

He asked if I was having a good evening. There were fine lines of blood in the corners of his eyes. I said I'd come to write a story while he was working. He frowned, but quickly, so that I wasn't completely sure that he had. 'Tell me about your day,' he said.

I searched my mind for something unusual to entertain him. There was a pause in the music from the parlour. The track changed. There were raised excited voices, and I imagined the trio on the couch jumping up to dance. 'I've been playing outside,' I said.

'I heard you, earlier. But I was talking about school. What did you do today?'

I told him some more about the book we were reading in English. He'd already told me that he'd read it when he was a young boy, much the same age as me. But now he'd forgotten the details. He'd read many other books since then, and his head only had so much room. I asked him how many books he'd read. 'Oh I don't know,' he said. 'I stopped counting them a long time ago. I'd say it must be at least a million by now.' He asked how the music lessons were going. We'd had guitar practice that afternoon, and Mrs Mac had lost her temper because Rothwell kept coming into a song too soon. 'Which one's Rothwell?' he said. The swimmer, I said. Tall Rothwell. Skinny, hates the guitar. That Rothwell.

He smiled. He asked if I'd been smoking. I said yes I had, a few minutes ago, with Otto and James, my mother's friends. I sometimes had a small glass of wine with dinner, and he knew my mother allowed me to sip from her drinks occasionally, so I didn't think there were any rules.

He stood and lifted me into his chair, and told me to wait in the study. 'We can read a story when I return,' he said.

He paused at the door, his hand on the knob, then came back and opened one of the desk drawers, handed me a pencil, and slid the pages he'd been marking to one side. He placed a blank sheet of paper in front of me, and smiled.

When he was gone I began to write, becoming lost in a land of ghosts and fairies and monsters. Here, overgrown pathways snaked through cold lonely misty forests towards enchanted cottages that glimmered inviting and warm. You knock on the door and they've been expecting you, and you wonder how they knew you were coming, and the inside is filled with pretty lanterns and candles and the enticing aroma of a baking cake.

By the time my father returned, I'd almost filled a whole page, but the story wasn't finished. He lifted me out of the chair, then sat down and placed me into his lap. He smelled cold, as if he'd been walking through a damp twilit garden. 'What have you been writing?'

'A story,' I said.

He looked as if he had forgotten that he should be smiling. 'What kind of a story?'

'It's a fairytale.'

'I enjoy hearing those kinds of stories. Would you read it to me?'

'But it's not finished.'

'It doesn't have to be. You can read what you've written so far.' This time he remembered to smile, but it was unconvincing, and I wasn't fooled. 'If you want to,' he added.

I read slowly, to lend the piece some atmosphere, and he relaxed beneath me. At one point I turned to make sure he was still awake, and he looked as if I'd caught him in the middle of something private. 'Carry on,' he said.

I'd almost reached the end of the page when the door opened abruptly. A woman was standing there, framed by the light from the hall. The desk lamp wasn't bright enough to reach her face. Behind her, the house was silent. At first I thought it was my mother's friend looking for the bathroom, and I felt my father's body stiffen, ready to direct her down the hall. But the woman spoke, and it was my mother.

'They've gone,' she said. 'Everyone's gone. Are you happy now?'

My father took me off his knee, and stood me on the floor like a giant chess piece. He walked over to my mother, and she raised a hand to her hair. 'Leave me alone,' she said, but he hadn't done anything. He grabbed the top of her arm and led her from the room. Neither of them looked back, and my father closed the door behind them. I wondered if I should follow, but sensed I was expected to stay in the study.

After a considerable time, I became aware of my father's woody cologne. I'd been resting my head on the desk, thinking about an ending for the story I'd begun, but I hadn't written anything more. He put the page and the pencil into the drawer. Tomorrow was the start of the weekend and I would be able to finish the story in the morning, he said. I was drowsy with the imagined, and not quite of this world anymore, and he lifted and carried me upstairs to bed. I undressed clumsily while he sat on the edge of the bed, and when I was ready he pulled back the quilt and invited me to get in. He kissed me goodnight and left.

***

I never asked about my mother's final party, or about why her parties stopped so suddenly. My parents never talked about it, so neither did I. Except once, years later, when I was much older, and had started going to parties myself. I was ready to go out one evening, and feeling restless, caught in that dead zone when it was still too early to leave the house. I asked my mother if she missed her parties. She was reading the evening paper in the armchair beneath the faded lampshade. 'What parties?' she said. She looked over the top of the paper, and I felt a momentary discomfort with her proximity to the self I'd chosen to exhibit for the evening.

'When I was at primary school. You sometimes had people over,' I said, withdrawing a little from the tightness of my jeans.

She looked away, as if to locate the memory in the corner of the room. 'They weren't really parties. A few friends occasionally, maybe.' She returned to my face. 'Why do you ask?'

I wasn't sure. I started to move away, towards the door.

She let the paper drop to her knees. 'I don't know,' she said, 'if I miss them. I've never given it much thought.' I told her I'd been recalling the last party. She became pensive, as if this might be the first time she'd considered the matter since that evening all those years ago. 'I suppose I grew tired of them.' She was old and detached in the glow of the lamp. She didn't return my gaze. She was inside some distant contemplation, and after a while I turned to leave. I heard her shake the paper out, and when I glanced back inside the room she had begun to read again.

THE STATUE

My elderly neighbour Captain Seevers is a kind-hearted type, always looking spruce from early in the morning, and with a way of talking that makes you feel as if the day's coated in soft caramel. It's the drawl he puts into words, slow and deep like he's got all the time in the world. He talks, and I listen, but I never really pay attention to the content, more the manner of his delivery. He always calls me 'young man', which I like, coupled with a loaded look, which I also enjoy, because I'm sure I'm not generally regarded as being all that young or compelling anymore.

And then I step away from him, because you've got to get on with your day. I step away, and go into the caramelised morning, trying to keep some part of his voice with me, the way you might try to retain a song in your head because it puts you in an easy frame of mind.

The other day when the morning was ended I stopped outside the library. I stopped to watch the lunchtime people sitting on the grass. I watched but felt as if I had nothing to contribute. These were the people doing the work. The students, for example: they always arrive with their books, and it's an hour till they have to be back in the lecture theatre or the seminar room, and they spend that time on the cool grass by the library, soaking up more knowledge.

While I was there, a couple of things caught my eye and aroused my attention. In particular, a boy sitting nearby. He didn't notice me, but I glanced at him a number of times. My glances became lingering but I was careful to prevent them from turning into stares. He was drawing onto a sketchpad, repeatedly looking from the pad to the statue looming over him. He was attractive. Shaved head, pierced ears, tight shorts that looked like swimwear. He had the serious pondering expression of one much older.

The statue he was studying was of a naked man. I thought that if he wanted to draw naked figures then I'd willingly pose for him, right there on the grass if he wanted and if we were feeling as daring as the statue. It was somehow twisted that he was drawing a statue when he could be observing and copying my body, alive with movement and responses and emotion.

I closed my eyes and rested my head back onto the soothing grass, and remembered how caramelly the day had been right after my interaction with Captain Seevers. And in that mood I decided that as soon as I looked up again, the sketcher would be gazing at me. He'd have put down his pencil, placed it behind his ear, or to one side on the grass, and he'd be smilingly taking in my presence, considering me for his next life study.

But this was all wishful, of course, and I knew it wasn't really going to happen. The boy would still be attending to the statue and the drawing he was making. He was that kind of person, I was sure. The focused artist. I've known the type. The art comes before all else, and the sex is a quick release and then they're eager to get back to their work. Go on, get back to your art, now you've released and got yourself spent and empty. Go back to your precious art and forget about me till you're inconveniently brimming with desire again.

And so I became convinced that when I opened my eyes the boy would still be absorbed in studying his statue, copying the lines of its cold stone penis. And the proximity of this boy and the naked form and my exclusion from the activity troubled me so much that I decided never to open my eyes again. Life, I concluded, would be simpler with face shut against the world and against the complex truth of this person next to me on the grass at the library.

When I did open my eyes, the boy, the artist, the person with the pencil, was nowhere to be seen. Gone, and with him the lunchtime crowd. It was me and the statue, and its eyes followed me all the way back to the street.

LONDON APPRENTICE

He woke alone in his single bed. Sounds of traffic carried from Holloway Road, and muffled voices rose from the street below his window. Gazing wide-eyed at the familiar damp stains and spidery cracks in the high ceiling, he summoned the energy to rouse his body from the cosy wrapping of sheets. Today he'd probably have to buy milk, bread, fruit, veg, the basics. He was down to his last few pairs of clean socks and underwear, so would need to visit the launderette before long. He pulled on yesterday's underpants, nestled his erection in the waistband, the head protruding, then slipped a shirt on. In the kitchen, he boiled the kettle for tea. The couple of slices of wholemeal in the breadbin were probably his.

While he was toasting, his housemate Dennis walked in, bug-eyed and searching. 'Don't forget the rent's due this week.'

Dennis, he suspected, was up to no good, might be fiddling the rent, creaming a portion off for himself. There was something amiss, anyway; he'd sensed it soon after moving in. And the rental contract was kept well under wraps. But what could be done? It was a shambolic house, and mercurial, and though there was good and bad in the arrangements, it was a place to live. He put suspicion out of his mind and spread margarine thickly on the toast, feeling Dennis's eyes all over his arse. He turned round. 'The rent, yes,' he said. 'Do you mind if I use a splash of your milk?'

Dennis nodded, then returned to his room and shut the door.

He wondered what went on in there. Dennis had said he was a musician, but no music ever came from behind the door. He sniffed the only carton of milk in the fridge. It was on the turn. He'd sort the rent out. He always managed to find the money when it was needed.

***

Inside the Angel tube station, vast cavernous interior, morning rush over, not too many people around, he clambered down and up the breathtakingly steep escalators, over and over, and enjoyed the sensation of plunging deep beneath the ground then resurfacing into the ticket hall. He'd been running at first, clanging the metal steps with abandon, but while hurtling down suddenly realised that one misstep, one slight miscalculation, could send him tumbling to the bottom. How easily everything would be over. So then he'd slowed his pace, walked the machines until breathless. Now he just rode them, holding firm to the handrail, and allowed himself to be carried in sweeping descents and ascents, mesmerised by the mechanical sounds and the rhythmic motion.

A public address announcement boomed through the air, plummy and resonant, asking for Inspector Sands to report to the control room. The announcement was repeated twice. A transport worker he'd encountered late one night in the gardens at Russell Square had told him that 'Inspector Sands' was code for a potential emergency. As the escalator plummeted once again he looked for signs of anybody or anything that might be a cause for alarm. He left the station when he noticed two assistants in the ticket hall regarding him with steely suspicion. Might he have been the perceived emergency?

***

The day was men-only at the Turkish baths on Ironmonger Row. It was quiet inside. He struck up a conversation in one of the hot rooms with the only other user, a man from Scotland who told of flying often into London on business. The nature of the business was not stated. The man described a drab existence, far from home: tedious nights in corporate hotels, packaged sandwiches and sour red wine for dinner in his room, the only company the television opposite the bed and the opening and closing of other room doors and constant clanking of the lifts. This, said the man, was why he visited the baths when he was in town. For friendship, and company. The man's towel inched up his thigh as he spoke, revealing more of a pasty interior skin.

They sat quietly for a while. Then the man, puffing and huffing, wiping fluids from his brow, said he was going to shower and cool down, and left.

Now alone in the hot room, he shrouded his face with his towel and thought back to an incident a few weeks ago. He'd been cruising the fiction section in Foyles, but had attracted unwelcome attention from a stuffy member of staff who seemed wise to his game. Rattled, he'd left the bookshop, emerging right into the middle of a late afternoon summer downpour, so had taken shelter beneath the arch on Manette Street. A man came towards him from Greek Street, eased his pace, folded his umbrella, walked past a little then came back and found an adjacent spot under the arch. Slightly out of breath, the man frowned at the thundery skies; talking sideways, he asked if business was slow with the weather being so inclement. 'Yes,' he replied with a quick laugh, unable to read the man's intentions clearly. The man appeared mature, yet not old, dressed in a youthful manner. More than that: his stature was upright and lithe. The man wasn't laughing, though, and carried within his presence an air of multiple possibilities. 'Yes,' he said again, having had a moment to consider the man's question in a more serious light, but still tentative, 'business has been slow. With the weather.'

Now he heard the sauna door reopening. The Scottish businessman, returned, dripping wet, bringing the refreshing scent of cold water into the room.

He replaced his towel across his lap, but not before he allowed the man the opportunity for a lingering look. He smiled at the man: if it was friendship and company he was after, he might very well have stumbled across the right person.

'What about you?' the man asked, taking up a closer position on the bench, hitching his towel as he sat, newly confident. 'Day off work?'

'My rent's due,' he answered, 'later this week.' He touched the man's leg and held his breath. Corporate skin. Cool and lonely, searching, moneyed skin.

***

On the way home he grabbed a six-pack at the off-licence near the station, then unbuttoned his shirt and ripped open a can as he strolled down Holloway Road towards the house. He had it in mind to lie in the sun on the grimy terrace out the back, under the kitchen window, to locate a patch of the tropics among the roof slates and television aerials. By the entrance to the house he spotted a group of youths, bikes and coats and belongings staking out a spread of territory. They fell silent and watchful at his approach.

The group's youngest member, a scruffy pre-teen boy with spiked dirty-blond hair, declared, ostensibly to his friends, that one day he'd like to try being fucked up the arse. None of his cohort reacted, though they waited amid sizzles of expectation.

He ignored the boy's outburst. Kept walking, unchanged pace, looking at anything but the youths, pretending not to have heard, or not to have cared. Nothing more was said or done. The tension fizzled, you could hear it, going the way of so many incidents that amount to nothing each day.

But he'd changed his mind about basking in the sun, aware the youths might somehow gain access to the terrace. He opened the windows of his room and, in shirt and underpants, watched the street, drinking one after another of the beers until they were gone and the afternoon had cooled into evening. With the softened light and early inebriation came some measure of ease and reassurance. The night ahead beckoned quietly.

***

A twilit dash across the field at the side of the houses. A shortcut to the shops. From out of the phone box near the shopping strip jumped a boy, maybe middle teens but it was difficult to tell. The boy made a noise low in his throat, like a growl, surely an attempt to elicit alarm.

He stepped back and away from the boy, a retreat, startled, perhaps a little unnerved.

The boy, laughing, delighted at his success, was alluring, dangerous, provocative, sure of himself and his actions, beyond his years.

Heart quickened, surprised at being shaken, and also relieved, though at what he couldn't identify, he crossed the road to the corner shop, bought a small bottle of vodka and a ready meal.

On the way back he entered the recently vacated phone box, lifted the receiver, heard the purr of the dial tone. Upon the mouthpiece was the scent of the boy's breath, sweet and smoky. He watched the traffic lights flicker from red to green to red again. He replaced the receiver. Then he changed his mind and decided to make the weekly call to his family, far away in the north, while he was still relatively clear-headed.

These despatches from the capital's frontline, as he saw it, followed a regular pattern. His mother said she'd been worrying about him. She asked about work, a job; how was he doing for money? He found himself staring at a sign above one of the shops: tax offices, first floor. He told her he'd found a position in a small accountancy firm nearby, full-time, doing routine but secure and adequately paid admin work. He was surprised at how glibly the story popped out.

Back at the field. The phone-box boy was sitting on the wall near the street. He was smoking; waiting for his dealer, perhaps, or a buyer or a friend. Or waiting to pick up some passing trade. Or just waiting. The boy let on, a nod, a cordial acknowledgement, no hard feelings, a faint smile released through the cigarette smoke. It was a mild night, and the boy had unzipped the front of his hooded top almost to his navel, revealing a bare torso.

He returned the smile, but guarded, sober, careful. Had the top, he wondered, been unzipped earlier, at the phone box? As he walked away, he knew, could feel, that the boy was watching him.

He paced his room like a nervy kitten. Vodka in hand, he stood in the hallway and stared at the closed front door. An array of adventures was occurring outside, beyond that door. He was thinking not only about him down at the field, doing by now god knows what, but also of all the boys and all the people and all the fields throughout the vast city. So many elsewheres calling. Time slipping by, opportunitiesblooming then withering.

***

After the ready meal, a dazzling scintillation of choice lay before him. The underground toilets at Piccadilly tube station were a possibility: an historic venue, known and hackneyed, a favourite of the older queens and tourists and out-of-towners. Or Liverpool Street station, crawling with drunken City boys at the end of the working day, suited and loaded and horny, wound tight and determined to find release, whether violent or sexual or both.

But he ended up near the underground toilet block at Shoreditch. Passed by, passed back. He was putting on a show of innocence for an old boy he'd clocked leaning on the railings on the other side of the road. He'd never seen the man before, and probably never would again after today, yet for some reason it seemed important not to appear calculating. Down the stairs he went, pretending he'd just realised he was bursting for a piss.

It could have been any time of day in that chamber beneath the streets. It was crowded, as if there'd been a call-out over the East End rooftops. This was the place to be. An epicentre in a city of them. All within that tableau were there for the same thing, really, when you boiled it down. Maybe some had come in just to use the toilet or to freshen their faces of grime from the traffic fumes, and a few had stayed on, liking what they'd uncovered. Such surprises can often be found underground. There was safety or security or something like it in the air. A sense of solidarity in numbers.

He found a spot at the long urinal, gauged the spaces, not too close, not too far away. He unzipped his fly, pulled out his cock, looked ahead at the porcelain. His left leg started to judder with nervous anticipation. He flexed his foot to fix it. He leaned forward slightly and took a look along the line of men. He discounted the fellow to his immediate right: not his type, suited and stocky and red-faced and giving off a whiff of desperation and urgency. Probably married, over-mortgaged, middle or senior management, wife and kids and dog at home in suburban Essex or Kent.

The man at his immediate left at the end of the trough was right up his alley, and was so close he could feel the energy radiate from his flank. This one looked like a slight-framed manual worker. Scuffed and muddy heavy-duty work boots, canvas pants too big for him. A genuine outfit, though, not a costume. He'd popped in for a quickie on the way home. He was what you might call straight acting. There was a squelch of chewing gum, spearmint mingling into the scents of cum and piss and bleach. The man must have been aware of being assessed, but he stared forever at the porcelain, deliberately nonchalant, his hand poised on his picturesque penis, motionless save for the slow rhythm of his jaw.

And then a clatter, and the group began to scarper. He turned round to see a cleaner with a trolley of mops and buckets and cloths and liquids. Flies were zipped, cubicle doors closed and bolted, faucets turned on, the crowd scattering in a hurry to a regular straggle. The cleaner began to mop in great sweeping swipes, slow and steady.

Thwarted, he went back up the stairs, startled at the shock of night. He blinked, stood for a minute. The old man across the road was gone.

***

He was often drawn to the council estates and shabby rental properties and edgy public transport to the east. Here stretched beautifully dismal swathes of tower blocks and uniform lines of terraced houses, porridge concrete and reddish bricks fugged by decades of living. Smells of over-boiled cabbage and cheap roasts on desolate Sundays. Piles of clothes and bric-a-brac left out to rot in boxes and crates in overgrown weedy backyards. He would kick litter as he wandered and wondered at the dramas within the homes.

He frequented lonely corners of Mile End, entranced by ghosts and history and otherness. The men were harder, more serious, mature, steeped in smoke and chemical fumes, with histories that had given them granite edges. The streets oozed a mildewed wisdom. This was a land of abandoned theatres, all-night grocery stores, caged off-licences and grubby takeaways, and of wide open roads. Cold and old, forgotten and beautifully crumbling. Working-class to the core, but the scourge of gentrification's creep was tearing at the fabric in parts, threatening to rip gaping holes in the place years down the line. Here was a dingy pub, around for donkey's years, where men in overcoats sat for hours over their pints, staring into the room or studying racing form or doing the crossword; two doors down, a cafe called Tisane sells fancy pastries and gourmet sandwiches, herbal teas and espresso coffees. For now, new and old lay in a precarious balance, the one not smothering the other.

He'd heard stories of noise and bother caused by local boys. He thought about this, and looked up at the hundreds of staring windows in the tower blocks. To him it was a beautiful scene, bathed in the special early evening glow of streetlights; serene, brooding. He crossed the car park and entered one of the buildings. A blended stench of yesterday's urine with disinfectant and chalky cement. He took his time in these places, hovering longer than necessary outside lifts and locked doors, and staring up dim stairways towards the next landing. He touched the front of his jeans, traced the hardening outline of his erection, cupped his balls through the denim. The only sounds a faltering light buzzing in the stairwell, and his own breath coming short and shallow, and yet he was sure someone was listening from the landing. He waited, waited, sniffed loudly.

***

He drifted through the streets, ever the flaneur, and ended up at the London Apprentice. An old staple, the LA; an important stitch in the fabric of the city's queer history, though the place wasn't really his cup of tea: too many leather queens and moustached clones, and a touch too much of the dungeon about it. But that night it was an easy option, close at hand.

While waiting to order a drink, he met a boy from Hoxton. Gaunt, his hollow face carrying suggestions of form with class A drugs, and sexy. They tried to talk, but it was difficult over the music. 'I want to show you off,' said the boy, grabbing his hand and parading him up and down stairs, along one side of the dance floor then the other, and then sailing through the middle. The boy kissed him as they tried to keep a rhythm, and put on a show of grabbing his arse as if everyone in the place was watching them, as if anyone else cared.

They left the club and walked through stained concrete underpasses lit in smoky orange. The boy stopped to piss against a tunnel wall. He looked hungrily at the boy's pale slim uncut penis. Soon his hands would be upon it, stroking, his lips around it, kissing and tasting.

They climbed several floors of a neon-lit tower block. The walls inside the flat were splashed and sprayed with slogans, graffiti, images. 'Don't say it looks like a squat,' warned the boy. But it did, though not in a bad way.

He undressed, stood naked and hard, but it was cold so he got under the sheets on the camp bed. The sheets were greasy and stained and smelled of stale skin and hair. But the other wasn't showing any sign of joining him, and instead sat at the table smoking and jittery like he was jonesing, and speaking once more of an ex-boyfriend he'd mentioned earlier in the club and again on the way here. His voice rose with indignation at the injustices of love gone wrong. Calling the ex a bastard, a cunt, a cunting bastard. The boy's eyes rolled and widened, his words augmented by the lit cigarette swiping through the air.

Too aroused to give a toss and with no counsel to offer, he wanted the boy to get it all out of his system and pipe down and get his kit off, but there was no indication this would happen imminently. He interrupted the tirade, said he'd just remembered something.

The boy stopped speaking, perhaps stunned by the suddenness of the quiet tones.

He explained to the boy that he was meant to call a friend, one of the guys he shared with. This guy was like the mother of their house, always anxious for the others, and would be concerned if he didn't hear from him soon. He took his watch out of his shoe and checked it for effect. 'Christ, it's late! I'm usually home by this time.'

The boy swallowed this whole, was tranquil again. 'There's a payphone right outside on the landing,' he said, and gestured to the front door.

And so he re-dressed, pocketing his watch discreetly rather than fumbling with the strap. He picked up his bag, hoped that wouldn't arouse any suspicions. Once outside, clear of the flat, relieved to have found the front door hadn't been locked – because that could happen; you never knew who you were going to run into – he raced all the way down the stairs, not thinking, not stopping to look back in wonder at what the boy was calling after him.

***

The streets were balmy and quiet. When he reached Old Street he peeled off his jeans and rolled them into his backpack and carried on walking in shirt, trainers and underwear. Further along he sat on a low brick wall bordering one of the rundown office blocks. He found an unopened packet of Embassy cigarettes in his bag. He unwrapped the pack and lit a cigarette, and considered the night.

A police car slowed down, so he fixed his eyes with benign distraction, steady and unhurried, and he could feel the coppers weighing him up, could sense the decisions they were coming to in the confines of their vehicle: shall we talk to this one, or leave him, let him get on with whatever he's doing at this time of night? The police viewed things in small and unimaginative ways. The car hovered as if about to stop, then sped up and drove off. Perhaps they'd been interrupted by their radio. Or were circling the block to check on him again. He'd still be there if they did, on the wall, and surely that would go some way towards satisfying them that he had nothing to hide.

He lit a second cigarette. He wasn't doing anything wrong, anyway. There were no laws proscribing the wearing of certain items of clothing in public. Underwear, outerwear, they were labels, it was all arbitrary. The law itself was arbitrary. Less than thirty years ago, he'd have been done for having sex with another man.

But what if the police came back? This time they might reach different conclusions. They might be bored and in search of a diversion. He'd heard stories. He doubted they'd be up for an intellectual debate. Was it worth the risk?

He was startled by shouting to his left, followed by howling laughter. Three drag queens were ambling along Old Street. High, boisterous, but contained within their own activity. 'Hello, love,' the nearest one said to him quietly, breaking out of the group dynamic as they passed him at the wall. He smiled back, and something light and airy filled his heart. Off they went in a cloud of flamboyance.

He lit a third cigarette, and tried letting his mind become blank. But this was difficult. Always difficult. Instead he was carried to a memory, of another time he'd felt a welcome surge in his heart. A few weeks ago. Or was it months? He'd shaved his hair, painted his nails red, lined his eyes, worn a pair of orange hotpants he'd found at a charity shop off Regent Street. Doused in Eau d'Hadrien, he'd gone into the West End, had danced and cavorted at Fruit Machine. At dawn on the way home, hungry, he'd been drawn to Smithfield. He sat at a table by himself in the old market pub, surrounded by workers in bloodied aprons, and had egg and chips and a pint of Guinness. At an adjacent table, a couple of hefty butchers had shown a brief interest when his food was brought over. The younger one told him enough of those breakfasts would put hairs on his chest. He offered the man a chip, and it was accepted with a quick nod, picked daintily from the pile and lifted between a thick finger and thumb, then eaten with refinement. He'd been delighted by this surprising clutch of delicacies tripping across the butcher's burly frame. The second, the elder, and gruffer, said no to a chip, then, 'You're a blast from the past.' 'The clothes?' he asked the man. 'The lot,' he replied, a smile suddenly splitting his face wide open. An affable observation, without judgement or disdain.

Now, the voices of the drag queens faded to nothing. The patrol car hadn't reappeared. He hoisted his bag onto his back and carried on vaguely homeward, smoking as he walked, a jaunt in his step.

***

In the grounds of the estates near his house he spied two men beneath the spreading branches of a tree, pants round their ankles, lower bodies glowing in the dawn light, fucking in full view of any residents who might be awake at that hour. Nightclub spill-outs, probably. He stopped to watch, and they noticed him and carried on without any acknowledgement or shying off or any attempt at including him. At first they reminded him of dogs, getting on with it, unconstrained by social mores. But then he felt like the dog himself, dismissed, shunted aside, made seedy and irrelevant, and he turned sulky. Miserable, this; utterly miserable. He skulked off home to familiar emptiness and dust and stillness, his disappointment a quick deep falling.

ANGEL

At school they called him Angel. He says the name has stuck with him ever since.

'But what's your real name?'

'Angel's fine. I don't recognise the other name anymore.'

'Why did they call you that?'

'Schoolchildren, they come up with names. It has no logic. Although nicknames can have a poetic quality sometimes.' Angel rubs his hands together, cups them and blows into them. His face has been shaved, speckles of stubble and soft eyes are framed by the dirty flaps of his hat. He has a scent of pale violets, as if he's showered recently. He hugs himself, hands clamped beneath his armpits. 'Tell me about the hotel you're staying in,' he says.

'Oh it's nothing much. It's a small place. More a seaside guesthouse, really. It's on the front, not far away. Just over there.'

Angel turns to look. But only the seawall is visible, and beyond it nothing but mist.

'It's got a handful of rooms, a small quiet bar. I haven't seen a single other guest since I arrived.'

'And the food?' says Angel.

'It's just breakfast each day.'

'How is it, the breakfast?'

'I don't know yet. I only arrived this afternoon.'

'Tell me about your arrival,' says Angel.

'My arrival?'

'What you did when you arrived in the room.'

'I unpacked.'

'How did you unpack?'

'The same as always. Slowly and carefully.'

'I like to know these things. I'm interested. You can tell me. Take your time.'

***

You can tell him, he says. You'd have to admit that he's got the kind of eyes you feel you can confide in. And that gentle trusting mouth. He doesn't seem crazy. Unusual, perhaps, to be so interested. People tend not to care anymore. But you've met enough characters in your time to know that this one's probably okay. So what if he was walking alone along a desolate stretch of beach in the middle of winter? So were you. So tell him about how you arrived in town, tired from your journey. You couldn't find any taxis at the train station so you walked to the guesthouse. It wasn't a problem, you knew the way, but everything looked changed from the last time. Faded, dilapidated. Many shops were closed down. Barker's Fish and Chips looked like it was still in business, but it was shut for the day. You passed the old wishing well at the end of the pedestrian shopping mall where every summer you'd throw a coin, close your eyes, make a wish. The same wish every time, borrowed from your father, for good health and happiness. But the well was covered in graffiti. Right across the front, the word 'resist' had been daubed in violent white letters.

A gang of teenagers was coming towards you. You moved well out of the way, stopping short of crossing to the other side of the street. But one of them came close and bumped your shoulder. 'Watch it, Grandad,' he said. One of the others laughed. You kept walking.

You got to the guesthouse feeling older than you'd ever felt before. Faded and dilapidated like the streets you'd just walked through. Standing in the doorway, catching your breath and watching debris being blown along the wintry street, you began to wonder at the wisdom of your decision to come away. There were no other guests in sight, but out of season that's only to be expected.

And then that swiping glance from the man at the front desk. It seemed to question your right to be there. He was doing his best to dismiss you professionally. And his wincing smile: so vapid, and perfunctory.

You checked in, gave the interaction your best shot, and the man was cordial enough, you'll give him that, but it was all for show, and not a wholly convincing one, and behind the slick facade lurked a hint of waspish bile. He wanted to process you quickly. You were an inconvenient interruption.

You took a mental note of the times for breakfast, and took charge of the room key. The stairs were steep, and there was no lift, and there had been no offer of assistance with the bags. They were small, the two pieces of luggage, but they became heavy as rocks as you climbed. Finally into the room. A decent room. It would do. It was just a place for sleeping, after all. A haven, somewhere to withdraw. Over to the window then, to wheeze and gaze over the drear of the winter townscape.

And then the unpacking. That reassuring control. Always soothing, to unpack, to set yourself out. It says you've arrived and you're staying, for now. And now is all that matters, don't forget. First, the smaller items of clothing into the top drawer of the dresser, then the rest into one half of the double wardrobe. An old habit, that one.

Then your books from the bottom of the bag. Onto the dresser, a pile of three, neatly squared with the edges of the furniture. A variety of reading: a collection of short stories, a slim well-fingered volume of poetry, a hefty dusty novel. And placed on top of these, your journal. A fresh notebook for the trip, because you have no idea how long you might be staying. Then, a stand back to take it all in. It looked good and neat. Satisfying. It's all you really need, you thought: something to read, something to write in. All the rest is extra, in many ways.

The bottle of whisky was bought specially for the trip. You placed it on its side in one of the drawers, and covered it with underwear and socks. And then you changed your mind and took it out again and stood it next to the pile of books.

On the bathroom sink top were two tumblers wrapped in plastic. You rinsed one out, then broke the seal on the whisky, poured out two fingers. You took the drink back to the bathroom. You arranged your toiletries into a neat row on the glass shelf over the sink. Unwrapped the guest soap, washed your hands. Flicked the lights on then off, on then off. Tested the shower. It was feeble and dribbled from scalding hot to lukewarm. No surprises there.

You fixed your hair, and examined the face in the mirror. The light was strident, but it was definitely you in the glass. And you looked okay. Passable, anyway. An attempt at a smile ended up more like a snarl, too close and too bright in there, so you shut it down as quick as you could. Remember your mother and her ideas about mirrors? How she'd catch you staring at yourself, and warn of the devil lurking in the glass? You believed her, always. Why wouldn't you? She wasn't a fanciful woman. And you'd spend ages staring into the surface and beyond, trying to conjure the presence she had warned against. Once or twice, you thought you might have seen something peripheral. A flicker, a dash, you couldn't be sure. You'd become unsettled. But that was then. That was then, and oh don't recall that now. Not here, not now you're on your own in this room. Turn away, close the door, forget about the mirror.

There was time for a lie-down. Of course. You always have to collect your thoughts before you can think about going out. Anyway, there's no agenda while you're here. So. A lie-down. Not to sleep, but just a rest. A little rest. It had been such a long journey after all. Tiring and tiresome. That change of trains en route had been a fuss. The clamour and choke of diesel in the interchange station, the feeling of being unable to escape, and the possibility of the second train becoming packed and noisy with new passengers while it was waiting to depart; all that shifting uncertainty had been unnerving.

But you can rest now, you've arrived. Lie back. Look at the ceiling, cracked and flaky, discoloured in patches. It could be damp, those patches. The walls, fingerprinted and grimy, are calling for a lick of paint. The room's seen better days.

Tell Angel about wanting to shut your eyes. To collect your thoughts, but it's also a way of shutting out the world. That's what you do, isn't it? You shut out the world. If you can't see it, it's not there.

***

Angel's eyes are closed, as if in sympathy. He is still, composed, serene. Maybe he's drifted, but his face is upturned.

'I've been talking a lot.'

'Carry on,' he says, without opening his eyes. 'I'm listening, carry on.'

***

He's listening. Of course he is. He wants you to continue.

Travelling, you've decided, is no longer the pleasure it once was. Settling into a new place can sometimes be a joy, but the uprooting from familiar routines causes a stubborn anxiety. This basic room will be a home of sorts now, for a few days or even a few weeks if desired. That was a soothing consideration.

As you reclined on the bed you thought about the time ahead. Just like you used to in the holidays in the old days. It's entertaining, isn't it, to look forward to glorious times. To see possibilities in the days to come. You might find yourself waking into a cold morning in this bed, and you might even have company. There are probably rules of the establishment to consider, of course. House rules about guests of guests. No unregistered visitors allowed, perhaps. His nibs at the front will be a strict enforcer, you feel sure of that. But should the opportunity arise, it shouldn't be a problem. Rules can always be circumvented. We'll negotiate that bridge when the time comes. If. If it comes. No, when it comes. Think positively! Imagine, then. Allow yourself the luxury, and picture a morning in the not-too-distant future. In this room. A morning so close you can touch it. You're moving carefully out of the bed, this bed, so you don't disturb the sleeping other. There's another — what a delight! And then you're standing by the window and waiting. You pull the chair to the window and sit. You don't mind the waiting, because there's something at the end of it. This promise is for the figure in the bed to stir. Look how the sheet has moved off his body in the night, revealing him. Watch, savour, enjoy the nudity; wait for him to come to and remember, remember your name, to remember the night before without any regret.

You jolted, sat up. You'd drifted. Enough of that daydreaming. It's foolish, unrestrained. Come back to the ground. Back down. Stabilise yourself. Look outwards instead, out through the window to the silent roll and surge of the sea. It's been a while since you've seen that sea. You've missed it. Tell Angel how you've missed it. Tell him how you tried to hear the water from where you sat on the bed. You'd smelled it on the way to the guesthouse, on the walk from the station, grey and salty and dangerous.

***

Angel is staring out to the body of water. There is a hint of a smile on his face, or maybe it's rumination. 'I wondered, when I first saw you earlier,' he says. 'You were the only patch of colour on the sand, through the mist. It reminded me of another time. I found a man on the beach once, near here. In winter, like now. He'd been swimming. He was unclothed and his hair was wet. His body was quite beautiful. I touched him and held him, but there was nothing else I could do. I knew he was gone. But his body held an echo. Later they told me he'd had a heart attack.'

***

That Hopper painting, it came to mind while you were sitting on the bed. You can't remember its title. It's of a solitary woman also sitting on a bed in a hotel room. She's half dressed and slumped at the shoulders in much the same way as you were. Does he know the one you're talking about? In the image, which hovers somewhere at the back of your eyes, the woman holds something. It's a piece of paper, perhaps. Or a pamphlet or a book. Her mood is ambiguous, her attitude to the held item unreadable. These details can't be clearly recalled, not exactly, not now. Is she looking at the item or merely holding it?

Sitting on that bed, you felt a lazy slump in your body. A sour melancholy lingering at the corners of your mouth. You lifted up your shirt. Go on, collapse your torso even more and see how withered you can make your body. It's unusual, maybe, this revelling in your own ugliness. But who cares when no one is around to see what you're doing. When you're unobserved you can try to see how easily the belly concertinas into fleshy ripples like lumpy semolina or cream on the turn. Skinny and flabby at the same time. It's disgusting and fascinating. Stare and let it become normal to your eyes.

But hang on. Bad posture won't do. Oh dear me, no.

That last, spoken aloud, had sounded a startling and strange note in the bare room. The voice lingered as if someone else were present. But it was surely just a trick. Put it out of your mind. This is supposed to be a holiday, of sorts. Cheer up. Lose the morbid thoughts. Now force those shoulders back, and push and stretch that spine up, and up. And see how, like magic, the stomach is restored to smooth flatness. It resembles that of one much younger again.

Angel wants detail, so describe the bed in your room. That's a detail. Such a tightly made bed. Tidy and fresh. On the nightstand, a lamp, a glass ashtray, and a chunky telephone, its green lacquer striated with scuffs and dark scratches that no scrubbing will ever remove. At the front of the phone a printed label is slotted inside a plastic cover. It details dialling information for reception, room service, the concierge. But this place, 'intimate' is how it might be described, surely has no concierge, and the availability of room service is doubtful. You only have to think of the man on the front desk and imagine the farcical situation of enquiring about the possibility of afternoon tea being brought up to the room.

You reach a hand towards the phone. It's about to ring, you're convinced. It holds within its aged body the potential of electrical impulses from future communications as well as the trembling resonances of calls from the past.

But you're not expecting any callers. No one even knows you've come here.

Pick up the phone, dial 0. 'Reception,' you get from the man downstairs. A smooth voice, quite pleasing despite everything.

'I'm sorry,' you said. 'A mistake.'

Then dial 1. 'Reception.' The same voice, with an edge. You hang up. The phone rings, shrill and strange. 'May I assist with anything, sir?'

Don't call me 'sir', you wanted to say. Oh no, everything is fine, you said. Everything is fine, the room and the bed, and you're happy with the view of the sea and the front.

Silence. You sensed the rolling of his eyes through the wires.

When the phone was back in its cradle, there was a brief inner chastisement for the inane conversation. The way you'd spoken had sounded old and formal. The man downstairs had already jumped to his conclusions; there was no need to give him more ammo. A resolution, then: to effect a reticent presence on the premises. Minimal interaction. Don't allow him at the front desk any more satisfaction.

Tell this curious boy, here on the beach, tell him all of this, every detail, for no reason other than his wanting to know.

***

'And then?' says Angel.

'And then, unpacked, settled in, I was ready for a walk. I wanted to explore again, to see the pier, visit the amusement arcade at the end. I thought I might have a whirl on the fruit machines for old time's sake. But it wasn't to be. When was it, the fire?'

Angel reaches into an inside pocket and produces an oblong tin. 'Cigarette?' he says, opening the tin to display a neat row of them.

'No. But thank you.'

He closes the tin. 'I carry them to be sociable. I don't smoke. Well sometimes I do, when I want to look a certain way.' His eyes dart up. 'It was my father's, the tin,' he says, putting it back in his pocket. 'The fire. It was years ago. I don't remember exactly when. The pier was supposed to be knocked down afterwards, then rebuilt. But there wasn't the will. No one comes here much these days. The amusements had been closed a long time before the fire. There's little point in piers anymore. You've been here before, then?'

'I used to come here when I was a child. With my parents, for our annual two weeks. Then later with a friend. It holds special memories for me.'

'The pier isn't safe now,' says Angel. 'But despite the wire fencing, it's been accessed.'

'By kids?'

'Young people.' He points up at the structure. His fingers are long and fine. 'See the holes in the fencing? It's reckless, but people get curious and climb up. It's an itch. It gets the better of them. Don't you think that's the case with some people?'

***

Angel described the way he'd come by his name. He'd been born with tiny features resembling wings protruding from his shoulders. The doctors had told his parents that though unusual, it wasn't an unheard-of condition. The growths were harmless, a redundant physical feature, they said, and nothing to be concerned about. But it was terribly significant for the child. He became withdrawn once he began to attend school, once his peers discovered his secret, and he was given to experiencing prolonged periods of acute introspection. He was excused from physical education and games on medical grounds. These days he recognises that his mind was the main issue rather than anything physical.

The wings grew gradually. Not by much, but enough for the boy to notice. The doctors had reassured his mother they would never get larger, and these same doctors looked him over as part of his regular medical checks. Each time, they stated that as expected there had been no change in the size of the features. The doctors were either misinformed or deliberately concealing. Angel got into the habit of measuring the wings himself each day, and he recorded the numbers, and the wings were changing, slowly, slightly. He still has those measurements in a notebook. He can't recall the doctors ever measuring, but then it was so long ago, and he was so young. But some details were clear to him. That the wings weren't growing was not true.

The doctors had their reasons. Doctors always have reasons. It's part of their training. He can see that now, and he had understood it to some extent back then. The wings never went away, but he learned to live with them, to accommodate them. He is embarrassed no longer, or not so much. There is little call for him to be naked in communal circumstances these days. But still, he can't help but feel there are parts of his life missing, that he has missed out on functions and activities that others take for granted. He notices these omissions occasionally. Swimming, for example. He sometimes watches people at the beach. He envies their carefree thrashing in the waves; the risk, the vigour.

***

'Would you like to see the wings?' said Angel.

'Only if you're comfortable,' you said, unsure of the right answer.

He took off his coat, folded it carefully in half, then stood and unbuttoned then removed his shirt and allowed it to drop to the sand at his feet. His chest was like translucent stone and blued with chill. His nipples had hardened and peaked in the icy air, like delicate pink flower buds. A line of hair, adolescently wispy, trailed down his stomach. His underarm hair sprouted thick and dark, violently sexual against the skin. The boy was utterly without inhibitions, and he lowered his eyes and allowed an unencumbered appraisal of his body.

Your erection nudged at your leg, straining the fabric of your pants. You adjusted yourself, pointed your cock up and out of the way. There was other business to attend to, and you watched and waited. The two of you, held in a still life. Your gaze tore in, relishing the unimpeded study of a stranger's body. It wasn't difficult to imagine him completely naked, to extrapolate the revealed details into an overall picture. Evidenced before you was the shape, length and slenderness of the legs, with only a layer of fabric, thinnest denim between his skin and the wintry air.

He shivered and put his shirt back on. 'You can understand now, perhaps,' he said, buttoning up then tucking the shirt inside his jeans, 'how difficult things were for me at school. Other children can be so cruel.'

'How did you cope?'

'I learned to deal with it. There are ways.'

But, 'I didn't see the wings,' you said.

'You had plenty of time.'

'Nevertheless. Show me again.'

'Not now,' said Angel. 'I wouldn't let anyone look at all, usually. Not even once. You're different.'

'How?'

Angel shook his head. 'Kindness, perhaps. I sensed it when I first saw you. An unusual kindness, manifested as ' He clapped his hands, then rubbed them together. He rejoined you on the sand, closer this time, hugged his knees.

'What do you mean about the kindness?'

'Leave it there,' he said. 'Don't butcher the compliment.'

***

Angel lived with his elderly mother just outside the centre of town. His mother was sick, sick with sadness. The company of others was no longer a pleasure for her. Her appearance disturbed her. Her legs were veined and misshapen. She'd once been proud of her hair, but it had become grey and thin and straggly, and so full of holding pins that she hardly ever had the energy to take them out to wash it. He'd offered to do it for her one day, but she bit his head off. She had become like this gradually over the years. She didn't like the way she'd turned out. She had entered a particular system of living, and was precise in her daily structures. That's how it had to be now, for her. There was no other way. And Angel had to observe her strictures. If there was some departure from the regularity, she became acutely anxious. 'I'd invite you back,' he said, 'in different circumstances. We might have had tea there. But it's difficult.' He stopped talking, apologised for rambling.

You assured him there was no need to explain. 'Perhaps we could go back to the hotel for something to drink,' you suggested.

The two of you walked in silence, the wind having got up in strength. The boy had a gangling lope. He looked down as he stepped, as if wary of holes hidden in the sands ready to grasp and pull him to the centre of the earth. He wore shades of blue, entirely blue. His windbreaker, battered training shoes and those old-fashioned jeans, like those of 1970s youth. Worn thin, and so tight they were like a pale blue skin.

You became discomfited as you neared the drab building, thinking that your choice of establishment might reflect some aspect of your character that you were reluctant to reveal. You began to make excuses, saying it was just a place to sleep while you were in town.

There was no one on the front desk. You climbed up to the room while, behind you, Angel chattered incessantly about the decor. You sensed some compulsion to commentate, a need to fix his situation in place and time. You wanted to ask him to be quiet, in case someone should be alerted. This was the kind of establishment where a door might crack open, a sliver of face appear, and the next thing you know the manager is up at your room, eyes darting over your shoulder, making sure everything is in order.

Inside the room, 'How old are you?' you said, opening the whisky.

'Old enough for that,' said Angel, nodding at the bottle.

'You mentioned school.'

'I told you I was finished with school.'

'It's just ... well, you know.'

'It doesn't matter to me,' said Angel.

There was only the one chair in the room. You moved a shirt from the bed and offered the choice to Angel, bed or chair.

He rested his shoulders against the headboard, legs hanging over the edge, feet on the floor. Then he lifted a leg and rested its knee on the bed, the foot dangling over the edge. He jiggled the foot.

These were dreary surroundings to entertain in. You went around, adjusting items on the dresser, squaring the tidy pile of books, switching on the floor lamp, easing the gloom. 'You can take off your shoes, if you like.'

'Sorry,' said Angel. He removed his shoes.

'Oh I didn't mean anything. I just thought you might be more comfortable.'

He put both legs onto the bed, straight out in front. He kept his socks on. You handed him a tumbler of whisky.

'You never notice these fancy places,' he said, looking at the room with no hint of irony. 'I must have walked past this building so many times. I suppose it's quite expensive?'

But you dismissed the question with a wave, saying you disliked talk of money. He nodded, satisfied with the response.

***

It's you and Angel in the room. Just the two of you in the world. There's more to talk about, but there's no rush, and for now you're both quiet. You end up side by side on the bed. How did that happen? The softening of the whisky, perhaps. The magical enabler. The radiator is turned up, right up, as far as it can go. You reach out and then across; clumsy, but you don't care, and you allow your arm to rest on the other's body. No resistance is shown, and no displeasure displayed. Undress me, says Angel. His voice is a gentle breeze. You do as he asks, and he does the same for you. He's pliant, his body is malleable, ductile. His shoulder is smooth, the skin so smooth, but there's a protrusion near the top. Allow your hand to linger there, fingers touching at the sharpness, the boniness, and look into his eyes. Is that it? you hear yourself ask. Yes, it's right there, he says. You've found them, say his eyes, and it's okay to hold, stroke, play, let your hands feel and accept the feature. He starts to apologise. It's ugly, he says. You kiss him, silence him. His mouth tastes of, what? What is it? You can't put a finger on it. He stretches out, hands behind his head so he can watch you, crosses his legs at the ankles. It's like he's lying in the park, taking the sunshine. Move your face lower, take a good look. Stop a while. There's time to pause. And before you go on, before you change what you're doing, make sure it's okay to continue. Of course it's okay, he says. There's something about him, so trusting. You sense that he's never going to say no, not to you, not to anything you do. It's not that he's unassertive. More that you're so vanilla, and what could you do that's offensive? Is that what he's suggesting? No matter. Think about it later. You keep on looking up, cautious, checking he's alright; it's a kind of rolling consent you're after. It's okay, okay, he says. Don't worry, I'll tell you if there's anything I don't like. And even in those words, there was no impatience. He was just telling you how it is for him.

You kiss his chest, so sweet and soft on your lips, and his nipples so firm. Take a nipple in your mouth, then close your eyes and hold it there, inside your mouth. You're like a baby, says Angel. You open your eyes, look up at him. Is he mocking you? He smiles. So content, he says; like a baby, sucking on its mother. He's just observing, you realise. Nothing, it means nothing, but an observation. So then after a while you move low again. To the stomach, beyond.

The room is darkened now. The curtains are closed, lights off. But the shapes are enough. And the whispers of breaths in and out. He lies still, allows you to be still. His skin is cool and smooth. Soft stone. Ha! What? he says. Nothing, you say. There's no such thing, you think, as soft stone. But it is. Cool gentle alabaster.

Everything is sensation. The two of you are under the sheets, and on the sheets, and there are no sheets, they're pushed away, and it's touch, and kiss, and feel and hold. The boy's hand reaches out and between. Show me what you like, he says. His face is inches from yours. The scent of his breath. What is that smell? His eyes are there. You can see right inside him. Tell me, he says, what you want me to do. And you take hold of his hand and guide it gently into place, just where you like to be touched, where you've always liked it, and you ask him to leave it there, to hold on, that's all, and you move inside his hand.

And then he says that he's able to come, just by being touched right there at the place you found on his shoulder. Touch me while you're kissing me, he says, and that will do the trick. It takes a while, he says. It always takes a while, but it will happen, he says. And he's right, it does take a long time, you lose track, but it's fine, it's fine to take your time. There's no hurrying here. And finally he shoots high onto his chest and neck and it hits your cheek and your arm too, and that look on his face, the release. What are you witnessing? And then it's astonishing, but he just touches your cock, he knows, he knows somehow, he touches once, so deftly, and you come right away, onto his stomach and chest, and then you both press together and mix into one. You could die right there, you'd be happy to, but you don't say that, better keep it quiet because he might have some ability to grant your wish.

And yet, 'Tell me what you're thinking,' says Angel.

'Nothing.'

You both breathe for a while, and around you the room also breathes.

'Tell me why you came here, to this town,' says Angel. Those eyes of his are pools of infinite sadness, full of knowledge and pain. It's as if he has all the answers already, and only wants it all confirmed.

***

What is it about him? He asks why you're here, in the middle of winter, in this town where there's nothing to do anymore. He asks you, and you find yourself wanting to tell him. He's a listener, but it's more than that. Maybe it's the eyes. He listens with his eyes. He doesn't get bored. Such interest is a rarity. So tell him everything. Why not? Maybe he'll say that you're mad. Maybe he'll tell you you're right to think the way you do. Maybe he'll just take it all in, absorb and make no comment, offer no opinions or thoughts.

Talk to him about how things have been recently. Longer than recently, maybe. That morning when you saw someone in the park ahead of you, through the trees, off the path. That was the first time. A figure at the picnic table, sitting on the table, up high, feet on the seat. It was just you and this other person in the park. You were convinced they'd been waiting for you. A groundless notion but you couldn't shake the feeling. Too much to drink the night before, you thought. Too much to drink makes you jumpy, that's all it is. You slowed down, and as you drew closer you could make out their clothing. A hood drawn up over the head. They were hunched and still. Your eyes started to water with the staring. But then, when you were almost at the figure, almost there, past the trees, it was gone. You stood at the table. It was a table, nothing more. Illusions, you rationalised. Apparitions. Tricks of the light. But it happened again, and again.

An ageing mind. You know that's what people would say. That's what friends would say, if there were any to say it. It happens to people all the time, they'd say.

But this is different. This and the other times. It's more than illusion.

Also: You're out walking, and you approach a corner. There's a sensation you can't ignore. A reluctance to go any further. A fluttering in the chest. High anxiety. A feeling that something is waiting round the corner, unseen, moving. That you will collide, and it will hit you with shocking force as soon as you are exposed.

You had your eyes checked. They were in good condition. Excellent, considering your age. The optometrist was surprised you had no need for glasses. Then a visit to the doctor. Everything was in order. Blood pressure, that was the only thing. A bit on the low side. Keep an eye on it. How? you wanted to say. How am I supposed to keep an eye on my blood pressure? The doctor asked if anything else was troubling you. You'd been holding your concerns in your mind for such a long time, but now you had the opportunity to articulate them, words failed you. You knew it was pointless talking to this person, this professional who'd learned all about life from a university course. You were, you realised, looking in the wrong place for the answers.

*****

The eyes were deep and unnerving. They were touching a place inside you. You glanced away. Looked at the side of his nose instead. It was easier. Anything was easier than those eyes.

The wind was rattling the windowpanes. You got out of bed, out of Angel's embrace, and went over to check the radiator. It was turned up full, though it had become tepid.

Back to the bed, but your moving had shifted the dynamic. Angel sat up and said he really should be getting back. He wandered to the window. He stood there picking bits of lint from the end of his penis, completely unselfconscious. He looked up and smiled. And then he laughed. You laughed too.

You asked if he wanted to have a shower. He shook his head. But the smell, you said. Life has a smell, he said. He said again how he had to be getting back.

'Will I see you tomorrow?' you asked.

'I don't like to make plans. It's difficult. Every day is different with my mother the way she is.'

Yes, yes, yes, your mother, you thought. Your fucking mother, she's got you right where she wants you. You almost said it aloud.

The boy looked wounded as if he'd read your mind. For a second you thought you had said it aloud, then realised he'd simply seen your thoughts expressed on your face. 'My mother's dying too,' he said.

***

A walk along the beach road. The rain coming and going and coming again. Drizzly episodes. And freezing. But you've always enjoyed walking in inclement conditions. A turn here and there took you out of your way, and soon the area was unfamiliar. It was less exposed off the seafront, and the weather was less fierce, quieter. You came across a small row of old-fashioned cottages with ivy growing thickly up the walls and windows, and tidy square gardens. Pretty cottages, all different pastel colours that had deepened in the wet. A cat jumped from the bushes at the front of the row and waited for you to get closer. You put out a hand, and the cat nuzzled it and made a low noise, and then you stroked its back. The skin beneath its fur was uneven and lumpy, not quite right. You withdrew your hand quickly, then started to walk away. The cat stared. It appeared to be a healthy creature. And so, to check, you touched it once more, this time feeling surely the lumps, hard, dry and peaked beneath the fur. Then you went back to the guesthouse, briskly, all the time holding the hand away from your body, at your side. In the room you washed your hands over and over in scalding hot water till they burned bright scarlet.

***

His mother is dying too. That's what he said. You're sure of it. You could have asked him to elaborate. But sometimes it's better not to ask too much. It can open too many doors. You allowed him to leave without probing. Better to keep it simple. However, now the feeling is here again. That unsettled feeling. Tell it to go away. But that's not going to work. It never works. The troubles don't listen to instructions.

Lately, details are becoming an obsession. Often unimportant stuff. Waking in the middle of the night with a start, needing to clarify some minor fragment. Remembering has become critical, and if something can't be recalled you struggle till your head aches with the effort. For that reason, everything gets written down. Recording onto paper. But it is all uncreative material: times, places, amounts of money; names, of people, books, and songs, and films. Snatches of conversation. It is a tendency to hoard, and it is making you sick. You've been troubled for longer than you can remember. It's possible you've never really been well.

A fragment of a story you wrote a long time ago comes back now: '...most troubling is the disturbance I unleash on myself'. Repeat this phrase over and over. Maybe it was written all those years ago to bring solace in this very moment.

With this in mind, you find the energy to doll yourself up, best clobber, full of intentions. Ready to face the world. A few swigs of whisky. That's better. And now for some old tricks: a smear of lipstick to lift the pastiness from those thin lips, a line of pencil beneath the eyes. And then a reviving spray of cologne, and with a sense of getting on with things, off you go into the night.

***

The Carters Arms at the top of the hill hadn't changed at all on the outside. You ordered a vodka and tonic, double. The bartender was bored and mechanical. Seated primly at a round table in the corner, you felt misplaced, unconvincing.

Twenty minutes later, the same drink was still on the go, ice melted, weak. You were pacing yourself. Keeping things elegant. You watched the punters trickling in and out through the doors. The place was slowly filling up with chatter and smiles and laughter. The busy noise of lives in action. This is the life. Is it? Is it a life, watching people who aren't interested? Observing but not participating? None of them looked over. Not a single one even gave you a glance.

Another drink, then. You tried some easy badinage at the bar. But the barman was having none of it. Fuck him, the prissy cunt. You knocked the drink back right away, wiped your mouth with your hand. This gesture felt aggressive. Careful, now. But you can handle it. Nothing to worry about. You ordered another to take to the table.

You crossed your legs and then you were more at ease. Here we are then. An older man, yes. We can agree on that. Let's say mature, though. Mature, but cared for. Slim overall, and youthful in outlook. Well presented. Dignified. Urbane. There's a word. Yes. Sounds good. Sip, nod, nod, sip. Watch it, now. Take it easy. We don't want you getting ideas above your station. Don't put tickets on yourself.

Oh shut up. What's the use of all this inane yammering? Shut up. Stop going on. No one cares about you or your slim or dignified or urbane or any of it. It's the booze talking, all of this. It's gibberish.

You finished your drink. Time to explore the toilets. Time to give the gents a whirl. To have some fun, like in the old days. Off you go, then. Off you go. Have some fun. No one follows you in, but that's okay. You're content to wait, to bide your time.

A brutal place this. Draughty and cracked and disinfected. Dripping water and mottled mirrors fogged with age. The lipstick has gone patchy and crusted in one corner of your mouth. Pallor and thin skin surround those eyes, but it's mostly the light. A hard light, in here, and tinged with sickly cosmic green. It's a terrible light, and lonely; the kind that can make you terrible and lonely. The fire of the spirit in your chest and belly has given way to a taste like acid washing at the back of your throat from the cheap mixer.

Effect a pose, then. Head up, shoulders back. But oh fucking god please don't pout whatever you do. It encourages those hideous lines below the lips. Deep lines from sucking on too many cocks and cigarettes.

Grab a paper towel. Wet it and scrub off the lipstick, then swill some cool water over your face. That's better. Dry your hands through your hair. Another old trick — it vivifies the cologne.

You stand at a urinal, avoiding the pools of piss on the floor. You hold your penis, and no urine comes. It's a youthful penis, belying the age of its owner. You stroke it, hold it, stroke it, it grows. There are no problems down there. You slide a hand up the front of your shirt, caress your chest, your stomach. A quick glance at the door, willing someone to walk in.

But no one arrives.

The ardour wanes. Anti-arousal. Then nothing, it's all evaporated, and you're left with a feeling of being slightly ludicrous.

Back at the mirrors. 'Let's go,' you say to your reflection, checking your flies, fixing your clothes, smoothing the hair, allowing that face to relax into something representing its true feelings. But look closer. Here is the face of a man you no longer recognise. Its features bear no resemblance to your inner life. The mouth is turned down, the nose lined with capillaries, the ears long and droopy like an old dog's. When younger you'd felt some connection with that face in the mirror, even though at times the connection was fraught. But now you're looking upon the face of a stranger. You place your lips onto the image in the glass, open your mouth, let your tongue play on the cold surface, fascinated by the disconnect.

Then the door opens and someone breezes in and past, blurs towards the urinals like they mean business. At last, some action, maybe.

***

Take your time. Don't make it too obvious. You don't want to appear desperate. Step back from the mirror. If you squint, you don't look too bad. You're always too critical. Give yourself a break. If only the light was a bit gentler. Smooth and pat your hair, straighten and touch your collar. There. Now, back to the urinals. Let's take a look at what's going on.

But there's no one there. One of the cubicle doors is closed over. Walk up to it, go on. The only noise is your slow footsteps on the tiles and the dislocated plinks of water. There's no doubt you're loitering, but there's nothing to lose. The cubicle door is ajar. He's left it open. Left it open, for you. Why else? Cough, shuffle your feet. Nothing too obvious or direct, but let him know you're interested. Then wait.

But nothing's occurring. Get closer to the door and listen. Nothing. Wait and wait, and move your foot against the tiles, scuff, cough again. Not a peep from inside the stall. You can't even hear any breathing.

You push gently at the door with your fingertip. It moves slightly to-and-fro. No response from inside. What's he up to?

Back to the mirrors, then. Wash your hands again. Run them through your hair. Stand back, turn this way and that.

Oh, what's the use. Might as well go back into the bar. Whoever it is in that stall, they're not playing. But hang on: you've got to know. You need to satisfy yourself. And anyway, he might be in some kind of difficulty. Drugs, say. What if he's not conscious? This is a matter of civic duty. You go back to the cubicle. 'Hello,' you say, and another nudge at the door. It moves inwards. 'Everything okay?' you say, pushing the door wide open. It hits the wall with a bang. No one's in there. An empty stall. But you knew that, didn't you? You knew no one would be there.

***

Someone has taken your table. One younger, thinner, aloof, booted, tattooed, legs crossed at the knee, looking down at the opened pages of a slim book. A poet or a thug, or both. You stand to the side and slightly over the man. Cough politely. He looks up, smiles, friendly enough, but goes back to the book.

You don't want to appear predatory, so you move away. You've no claim on the table, and your empty glass has been moved to the window ledge.

Jostle, jostle, at the edge of the room. Keep an eye on the door to the toilets. Maybe you got it wrong. But no one comes out.

There is nowhere to hide in here. The room is too open and bright. You toy with the possibility of another drink. But no, it is time to leave. At the door, you turn to the barman and raise your hand, about to wave, but no one is looking your way, and your departure goes unnoticed and unacknowledged.

***

Nowadays there's a feeling of always looking out. Trapped inside yourself. Everything happens around you. This became your life at some point but it's difficult to pinpoint when things turned.

You wonder if Angel might be down at the beach. If not, someone else is sure to be down there. But the someone else might be after money. There's no way you're going to pay for your company. The alternative is to sit here in lamp-lit drear till the sun comes up, hoping for someone to walk down the street and happen to glance up at the lighted window, to signal a willingness to engage.

The framed sky is low and phlegmatic, as if filled with dirty snow. Debris is lifted and thrown along the beach road in eddies of grit. Further out, unseen waves advance onto the beach as they will forever. Some things won't change. If you stare hard and long at the pier, it appears to have flickering movements across its surfaces.

A trick, of the distance, of the moonlight. Shimmering wood. Possibly. But it is also possible that gangs have clambered up there.

'What are we to do?' you say to the chair in the corner. You shouldn't have done that. The sound of your voice has given you a shiver.

Outside the door, a faint shuffling across the carpeted hallway, as of someone dragging their feet. A heavy sigh, not far from the door. Another guest, perhaps. A new arrival struggling with their bags, figuring out the order of the rooms. The sounds retreat, and then return, stopping right at the door. Hold your breath, as if the breathing might be heard from outside the room. As if it would matter. The sounds retreat again. Everything returns to quiet.

You rise too rapidly and the room pulses, throwing its features into relief. You put a hand out to the wall but it isn't necessary. Blood pressure, that was all. Keep an eye on it. Indeed. And then, as suddenly as it had vanished, the gloom returns and spreads. Quick forks of lightning spark silently at the edges of the sea like lizards' tongues.

***

You switched on the lamp at the side of the chair. Its frilled shade, floral and comforting, brightened the room. The effect around the edges, however, was to create disarming shadows. You examined your face in the window glass. Reflected, your skin was smoother. Youthful and dewy, more handsome, like an earlier version of yourself. Certain tones of reflected light can be kind to a man of your age and sensitivity. You smiled at this, but the smile had a menacing tone inside the glass, reminding you once more of your mother's superstitions.

You watched a couple on the beach side of the street. A brisk man, and a woman with a plodding gait. They could have been lovers. There was a drizzle in the aura of the streetlights, and the wind was gusting. The two were stopped beneath the greasy light of the lamp opposite, and were trying to keep an umbrella from blowing inside out. The brolly resisted their efforts, and suddenly the man hurled it right over the wall, and it disappeared onto the beach below. They could have been laughing, finding easy humour in the circumstances. Or she might have been telling him that he should have bought a more expensive umbrella. Maybe he was telling her to fuck off, that umbrellas were a waste of time and money, that he'd only bought it because she'd insisted. Just then the man looked up, directly into the window, right into your face, and the two of you remained locked. But it was disconcerting. You withdrew from the window.

When you looked out again, the couple was gone.

***

A walk along the seafront. The night is abandoned, save for the occasional car. You see movements up on the pier. A group, loitering, having transgressed the wire fencing. There may be more people in the back, inside the abandoned cafe and offices. A solitary figure is at the edge of the fence, smoking, looking down into the shadows. The smoker spits high in an arc, out over the edge of the pier towards the sand or the sea, and his gob phosphoresces briefly and beautifully in the moonlight. Bodily secretions. Soon, you imagine, they'll all be drunk and high and pissing over the edge. They'll congregate in the blackened shell of the amusement arcade. They've spent so much time in each other's company that they feel comfortable occasionally masturbating together, and sometimes this activity breaks free of its boundaries so that one or another holds the penis of a friend, to help him out, and maybe even takes it into his mouth. And it means little to them, this, or it means little to one of them, but the other likes it, maybe. The other waits for it to happen, wants it, wills it along each time.

There's a hole in the fence. An opportunity that sets your body sparking. You walk towards the underside of the pier. Someone is laughing, the pier boys perhaps, but in such a far-off way that it must be some private joke, nothing to do with you.

Rest on the sand, just for a minute, to ease your eyes. Foolish perhaps, but you've exhausted yourself. Your mind has begun to play with an elusive mystifying thought. Your hands and feet are numb, teeth chattering, but you've no regard for the physical. You feel blissfully distant. Sleep, then wake. Dozing and waking, over and over. You could stand, to explore or to go back to the guesthouse. Here you lie, on the sand, fully clothed, middle of winter, and all the time the bed you're paying for is empty, going to waste.

***

A strange dream: A single sustained intense whale of a wind comes in the middle of the night while the town sleeps and the beach is the domain of night people. The gust shakes the frail remnants of the pier loose and pushes them away and along the beach, so that in the morning nothing remains but low blackened stumps, and children ask, 'Where did the pier go?' The adults do not know what to say, because they don't know what happened, but the children persist, insisting on an answer. So eventually the adults come up with a story, and they tell the children that the pier blew away. It was there one day, gone the next. In different ways, neither the parents nor the children have any confidence in this explanation, each certain that derelict piers, though brittle with fire damage, don't blow away in the middle of the night.

The images hover, out of reach, dark and unnerving. Bleak like the damp cold undersides of disused piers. Dreams are just echoes of the mind, you know that. Just images lingering in the recesses. The after burn of experience.

And then: a deep acridity of cigarette smoke and sour body odour. And a voice like gravel. 'What have we got here?' it says.

You open your eyes onto two figures silhouetted against the purple sky.

'Some old tramp,' says the second one. 'Or a faggot out for some rough trade.' The first steps closer.

From behind, another voice. 'Leave him alone.' Few words, but enough to know the speaker is gentle and whispered, and familiar. And though this third person isn't visible, you know their eyes are full and sad and knowing.

The first two stiffen. 'Fuck you,' they say.

And from behind, the third voice again: 'I said leave off, you cunts.'

'Angel,' whispers one of the two. 'Let's go,' and the two walk away. 'Fucking freaks,' they shout over their shoulders. And then they're gone.

'It's cold here,' you say. 'I lost track. I think I fell asleep.'

Angel helps you up off the sand. You face each other. He begins to undress.

'What are you doing?'

He says nothing.

'You'll freeze to death,' you say.

Then he's naked. He pulls you into his arms.

Inhale the familiar body. Then feel yourself wrapped deeper and further, as if being surrounded by heavy fabric. And there's another smell, musty and not entirely unpleasant, but unusual, earnest. This scent is like the inside of a box that's been sealed for a long time. Open your eyes, try to place your hands onto his back, to locate that sweet spot on the shoulders, but you can't move your arms, you're immobilised, enveloped. You try to speak, but there's not enough space to draw breath. It's warm and safe, but too much of both.

***

A memory. Something beyond, out of reach at first, then gauzy, flimsy, and then it's there, present, distinct. One morning a bird was floundering at the edge of the path in the park. A baby bird, it was broken, unable to fly, distressed. You picked it up, rescued it, and it panicked, tried to struggle free, and would have fallen to the ground and perished had you not placed your other hand firmly over it, cupping it, protecting it. You walked slowly, taking the creature home via the quietest route. You wanted to give it food, water, shelter, safety. The bird became calm. You stopped and carefully lifted your hand to check. The bird, in your palm, a small thing blinking up at you. You covered it again, for its own good, in case it should try to jump free. You carried on, gently. When you got home you opened your hands and the bird spilled out motionless and unblinking and lifeless.

Acknowledgements

I began writing these stories in 2007. Along the way I've been fortunate to receive much support, encouragement, and advice, all of which has contributed to the development of this collection. I'm very grateful.

Thanks to:

Andrew John Kaye for listening, for reminding me of what's important and, crucially, of what isn't.

Fellow Elwood Writers Jennifer Bryce, Margaret McCaffrey and Helen McDonald, there from the start with a collective wisdom I treasure.

Publishers, editors, judges, and others who've supported my work. *Overland* and Victoria University for their Short Story Prize. The City of Melbourne and its libraries for the Lord Mayor's Creative Writing Awards. Philippa Armstrong and everyone at Roomers. Tim McQueen and the Vision Australia Radio team for supporting new Australian writing and exposing mine to new audiences through the airwaves.

Kathryn Macdonald for guidance with my funding applications to Arts Victoria, now

Creative Victoria, and for encouraging me to keep trying.

All at Varuna, the National Writers' House, for warm welcomes, impeccable hospitality, and a cohort of new friends.

Carol Major for insightful readings of the stories and the connections between them; our conversations during my Varuna Fellowship and beyond have been invaluable.

Kate Goldsworthy for solid readings and considered observations during this book's editing process.

Barry Scott and Transit Lounge for believing in these stories and turning my manuscript into a book. More than ever we need small and independent publishers to thrive, so they can continue to enrich the literary landscape by reflecting the wider world and representing voices that might otherwise go unheard.

Versions of some of the stories have appeared elsewhere:

'Their Cruel Routines': winner, *Overland* Victoria University Short Story Prize; published in *Overland* 221 Summer 2015 and online at overland.org.au

'The Ministry Man': commended, *The Age* Short Story Award; broadcast on *Cover to Cover,* Vision Australia Radio, 26 January 2018.

'Twitch': winner, *Dazed* short story competition; published in *Dazed* Spring/Summer 2014 and online at dazeddigital.com

'The Americans': special commendation, Manchester Fiction Prize.

'Phase': broadcast on *Cover to Cover,* Vision Australia Radio, 1 September 2017.

'Playful Arrangements': published in *Roomers* #59 Spring/Summer 2015.

'So Much Lemonade': highly commended, the Bridport Prize; published in the *Bridport Prize 2013 Anthology* (Redcliffe Press Ltd); broadcast on *Cover to Cover,* Vision Australia Radio, 5 May 2016.

'Hot Spell': broadcast on *Cover to Cover,* Vision Australia Radio, 11 January 2015.

'Broken Rules': prize winner, CAE Short Story Competition.

Barry Lee Thompson was born in Liverpool in the UK. After studying art history at the University of East Anglia, he moved to London. He currently lives in Melbourne's west, Australia. His stories are published in Australia, the UK, and the USA, and have been recognised in awards including the Bridport Prize, *The Age* Short Story Award, and the *Overland* Victoria University Short Story Prize. His work appears frequently in *Roomers* magazine. He is a member of Elwood Writers, and of the Alumni Association of Varuna, the National Writers' House. Visit barryleethompson.com for more information.

Broken Rules and Other Stories is his first collection of fiction.

www.ingramcontent.com/pod-product-compliance
Lightning Source LLC
Chambersburg PA
CBHW011119050726
47495CB00020B/2806